How to Kill an 8th Grade Teacher

Wolf Redboy

Nine Mile Books

Nine Mile Books(USA) Inc., 110 E Broadway St., Ste. 206, Missoula, MT 59802-4592. U.S.A. First published in the United States of America by the Nine Mile Books Press, a member of the Nine Mile Group (USA) Inc. 2013 Published in Nine Mile Books 201. This is a work of fiction. Names, characters, places and incidents either are products of the author's imagination or are used fictitiously. Any resemblance to actual events or locales or persons, living or dead, is entirely coincidental.

Cover Design by Dariusz Janczewski

ISBN 13: 9780615640938
ISBN: 0615640931
Wolf Redboy

For the teachers.

ACKNOWLEDGEMENTS

I would like to thank all of my friends who helped me to make my book: My editor, Lacey Hawkins, thank you for your BRILLIANT thoughts and laser-like editing skills. Chris Nicholson, my wife if you were a woman, (it's still not too late). Scott Duthie – I can't even say. It's too much. You're family to me. Aaron Nicholson, for being a great friend, brother, and visionary/evolutionary X-Man. Mel Ewing and Larry Tarver, for being true Jedi Knights - thank you for our great talks and walks. Don't read this book, there are cusswords on page 38, 39, 40, etc. Janet Weertman, you are one of my dearest friends, and just to be around you makes me lucky to be hanging with a psychic/visionary/astrologer powerhouse. Katy Evans and Darius Janczewski– I can't put into words what you mean to me – thank you for your support. Alan and Nancy, don't read this book (thanks for being my second family, and reminding me who I am). Karen Rice, for being a kick ass boss with true leadership powers. Glenn Kreisel, for letting me have the RS job even though I was a literature major. Greg Lenihan, I'll never forget student teaching under the greatest high school teacher in Montana. I remember kids waiting after class to shake our hands, thanking us for the great classes. Paul Lenihan, for your constant enthusiasm, incredible energy, compassion, and talent. Bob and Jean Pettit– thanks for making Marie - and coming over to constantly light my house with your love, warmth and beauty. Shmedley Maynes – thank you for being the most important person in Missoula right under the mayor. Rebecca, hi sis! I love you. Thank you Sam for being a true friend, and taking me through the battlefields. Thank you Ben Anderson and congrats on beating the Octopus at the tournament. Love you, Ryan, I'm grateful to have the best brother in the world. Love you Dad – you made me who I am today. Thanks for your intellect, judicial powers, great oratorical skills, and open-mindedness, which made me who I am. Not to mention that sense of humor. I'll never forget watching "Rambo" and watching you laugh at the screen. It was like when you framed that picture of Nixon dancing to ballet in the bathroom. So it's your fault. And Mom's. Thank you Steve Saroff, for changing my life. You inspire me and make me better, and it's impossible to tell you the impact you made on my life. I'd like to remake "It's a Wonderful Life" with you as the star. That aside, you're a dear brother to me, and thank you for your constant encouragement, bravery, and great beauty as a person. Thank you Val, my favorite 3rd and 4th grade teacher. And Gary! My godparents, I love you both dearly. Look at what you've created, an insane person. Don't read this, Val. And most of all, Mom, my greatest teacher I have ever had. You were there for me every day of my life. Mom and Dad, my world, I thought of you when I wrote this. And finally, to my beautiful wife Marie, and my lovely kitty Sophie, you're who I wake up to every morning and you're who I am with all the time – I'm so lucky to have such support and unconditional love! Thank you all. You're my core.

CONTENTS

"I accept chaos, but does chaos accept me?"
-Bob Dylan

"If your parents like it, then it isn't any good."
-Charles Bukowski

PART I

Chapter 1

THE DESCENT

8.10.06

It was sweet of Ed to drive down with me all the way to Las Vegas. It really was. Especially because he didn't have much time left in the States. Soon he'd be going off to Iraq to report on the war for the *New York Times*. So I wouldn't be seeing him for awhile. It was sad, but all the same, he had no business commenting on the smell in my car.

I gave him a *look* and rolled my eyes back.

And the conversation continued like this for about 1200 miles.

"No longer are you a student at some college," Ed said, opening the window. "Now you are a teacher … This is a big step for you."

"Yeah, I know," I said. "But you know me. I really want to be playing music. As I always talk about. But, on the other hand, you're right. At least this will be a nice stepping-stone toward the rock band. Sting was a teacher."

"And Vegas will be cool, too," he said.

"Do you think?"

I looked at him. He looked away.

"Listen," I said. "Just so you know, *the idea of Vegas makes me want to vomit*. The only reason I took the job, again, is because of my dad. He likes the heat. And they're desperate for teachers."

"Sure, Las Vegas man, is a city that is growing like, what did you say, 3,000 people per month?"

"Yeah. 3,000 new people per month. That equals 30 new schools per year. And they have a huge budget because of the gaming industry."

We looked out at the passing mountains. Sharp and jagged brown rocks were everywhere. A dead animal was on the road being picked apart by lizards. A condor flew overhead.

I continued, "And it's true I knew that it would be easy to get a job," I said. "Why apply everywhere when you get can paid 50 grand – which is so much for a teacher - in Vegas?"

"Maybe there's a reason they're paying so much."

He stared ominously.

"Don't say that. Believe me I would rather not be in fucking Vegas! I want to be in Portland."

"Oh, I'm just joking," he said.

"No you're not. You can't believe I'm moving here. And I can't either."

Suddenly, I felt my legs paroxysm. My lungs tightened. "Please somebody shoot me. I don't know what I was thinking."

"No," Ed interrupted, patting my back. "It'll be cool, man. Think about it. It's a city of two million people. Two *million*. That's a lot. There's gotta be people who are just like you there. Think about it. I mean, there's the strip, right, but people who actually live in Vegas never go to the strip, I hear. It's a completely different world. I don't know why you're not more excited."

"I just feel like I should be up in Portland, driving pizza, following my bliss, and slaying my inner dragon."

"Well you can do that here, too," he said.

"Do you think so?"

"Are you kidding? Of course! And think of the women!"

"Yeah I know."

"So just imagine what it will be like in Sin City! Imagine what they'll ask you to do!"

"Yeah," I said, relaxing a little at this news. "That's a good point."

"It's heaven," he said. "A virtual nirvana."

I smiled. "Yeah, what was I thinking? I guess you're right."

"Yeah man," he said, his voice building. "All that money you're going to make. Fifty THOUSAND dollars. Try to imagine."

"Yeah." Curls of ecstasy ripped through my body. "I couldn't afford a cup of coffee and I got all those women. Imagine what it will be like if I have money for the first time."

"I'm telling you, man."

"You're right, you're right, Ed. As usual. This is going to be awesome. Get the band going, meet all these beautiful women …"

"YES!"

"…Teach, which is such an ethical thing to do."

"You couldn't pick a more ethical thing to do."

"This is going to be amazing."

Ed rolled his window down, even more.

"Does it really smell in here?"

"No," he said. "It's fine in here."

8.11.06

The lights were riveting. Ed and I pointed and laughed like little school girls. Elton John! Celine Dion! Jesus Christ! Of course in between being awed, we philosophized on how these great temples are really nothing more than monuments for losers.

"You won't catch me dead in one of these," I said throughout our conversation, referring to the casinos. Ed quoted Ozymandias. But that conversation encompassed maybe three percent of our total air time as we tried to figure out some way to find the hookers.

"ED! BACK OFF!" I screamed angrily, tearing at the newspaper that held the phone numbers of the pimps. Those newspapers were everywhere, apparently.

Unfortunately, we soon found out we couldn't afford any high class women, so we decided to settle on going grocery shopping for Fiber All instead.

We drove into new my apartment complex and met up with my new roommate, Colin. Colin was from Montana, too. We took the same classes together back in Missoula while getting our Master degrees. Those teaching classes where you learn words like *constructivism* and *scaffolding*. Worthless words.

But Colin wasn't like me. He liked those classes and he memorized scaffolding instead of going home to do something useful like … well, maybe, I don't know … learning how to become the GREATEST MUSICIAN ON THE PLANET.

So it wasn't a surprise we never really hung out back at the alma mater. We barely saw each other's faces.

But, seeing as we were both going to Vegas to be teachers - he called me up out of the blue and asked if I needed a roommate in Tinseltown. And I was like, "Yeah." He was gonna be a band director, and since I was gonna be an English teacher, it just seemed apropos to join forces.

He even helped me unload my trunk. We stood out there in the parking lot. "So, Leo," he asked, "where are you teaching? What area?"

"I don't know. Eastside somewhere, I guess."

He looked awkwardly at the ground, smiled softly, and then shook his head. "You're on the Eastside?"

He again shook his head.

"Stop shaking your head," I said. "Why are you doing that?"

"*That's ghetto*," Colin said.

I looked at Ed. "Oh great."

"It won't be *ghetto*," Ed jumped in, trying to keep things positive. He reached into the trunk and grabbed a box of cereal. He threw it at Colin.

"You tried this, Colin?" he asked. "It's Fiber All. We men should really be thinking about this, considering we're at risk for colon cancer."

"Don't try to change the subject, Ed," I said.

Colin shoved his hand right into the box of cereal, contaminating the entire bag. "Mmm ... good," he said. "Try some, Leo."

"No thanks. I prefer to eat my cereal from a bowl with a spoon."

"This cereal will create nice, perfect stools," Ed said, raising one finger in the air. "In fact, it *rakes* the system. Leo, you know Patrick, my brother?"

"Yes."

"Well he walked into the bathroom one day after I had taken a shit and apparently I had forgotten to flush the toilet, because when he saw the size of my crap, he actually asked me if I was a homosexual. Can you believe that, Leo?"

I thought about this information. "What is the name of that cereal, Ed? Here, hand me the box."

"It's good," Colin said. Crunch crunch. "Good."

"Fiber All."

8.12.06

It was tearful saying goodbye to Ed, but I was excited to start my new life. And Colin said he would never be home because he had a girlfriend, so I had this kingly apartment all to myself. Within our walled complex there were three pools, a couple Jacuzzis, a tennis court, and a security guard for safe measure.

"I think it's a perfect location," Colin said. "It's right next to the strip, and it's in between both of our schools."

Chapter 2

A CLEAN, WELL-LIGHTED
COMPUTER LAB

8.15.06

I drove for hours looking for the school building. And when I finally found it, I saw that it resembled a giant aluminum tin can of some kind. Coated in steel, the windowless structure looked like it had been dropped from a helicopter onto the ground.

This school looks like a giant tank, I thought, walking up the driveway. But when I went inside, I instantly recognized the smell of middle school. There were donuts and croissants sitting on a giant table with a sign that read: "WELCOME NEW TEACHERS."

I poured a cup of coffee and went into the library. Here, all the teachers sat in a circle and were assigned to write their histories on tiny index cards. Each teacher stood up, one at a time, and smiled before their future administrators.

"Hi, I'm Vitor Morales. I'm your history teacher. I'm from Arkansas."

"Hi Vitor," everyone said.

"Can you tell us what you wrote on your index card?"

"Oh yes," he said, frantically searching his breast pocket. "I enjoy hanging up posters, getting my grades in on time, and keeping to myself."

At this, he looked over at me.

Amidst this first day of "getting adapted to our new environment", we all got to know one person, and that was the vice principal. Her name was Patricia Davis. She was the one who hired me from up in Montana. I'll never forget the day she called me up in Missoula.

"So understand that we need some teachers - would you like to come down?" she had asked me.

"I would."

"The school's a little rough around the edges," she continued. "It's the students …but it's nothing to worry about."

"Well, I have a Master's degree."

Her voice was quivering, nice and raspy.

And now, I saw a Latina standing in front of me, dressed in a thin black mink coat, all curvy and vivacious. She was as beautiful as her voice had hinted at.

"I'm very excited to see you perform for me, Mr. Heffel Heffla heffer …" she said.

"Heffelapfle."

Her handshake was quick and strong. And there was something about her odor that reminded me of something … yellow and sweet. *What was that?* No matter. She was standing before me with her shiny black suitcase and display of pens and pencils. I couldn't help but to wonder … *Was there something between us?*

No. I shook my head. I couldn't allow myself to think this way.

However, at the end of the day, she surprised me out in the parking lot as I headed out to my car.

"Excuse me, Mr. Heffelapfle," she said. "You forgot your itinerary."

I smiled as she handed me my papers.

"Would you like to, perhaps, get some coffee, sometime?" Her voice rattled softly as she drew herself in, perhaps to signify that a more intimate conversation was about to begin. "You know ... to discuss teaching?"

I stared at her.

"No. I can't," I said. "Sorry. I just moved here. I gotta focus. But this is going to be a fun year." I closed my car door, and then rolled down the window. "I'll talk to you tomorrow!"

She blinked, still smiling.

She was a cool lady, I thought. But it was more important to focus, as I said, because I had a lot to do.

8.16.06

I got the key to my classroom from Bamby Robinson, one of the secretaries. She sat at her desk watching "The Fantastic Four" from behind a steaming coffee pot. Her five-year-old kids were leaping and playing on the office carpet, yelping like dogs. "You are in room 445B, Mr. Heffelapfle."

One of the kids ran into my leg.

"Cool. Where's that?"

"I don't know."

She pulled out a red rectangular photocopy of the building, and handed me a magnifying glass. After much squinting, we discovered that my room was actually the old computer lab.

"That will be nice," a disembodied voice said from behind me.

I spun around, only to see a short, stout, and forceful woman standing in front of me, her legs cocked to either side. Her hair was long, curly, and graying – and her skin was weathered and pink.

"Hi, I'm Anne Marie Feihr." (Pronounced "Fear".)

"Leo Heffelapfle," I said.

"Mr. Heff Heffel ... "

"Apfle."

"Heffersnapple. Well isn't that nice. Here, follow me. I'll show you where your room is, neighbor."

Bamby-the-secretary thanked her peer with a clandestine head nod.

I followed Anne Marie down a never-ending labyrinth of tunnels. *This is certainly a long way from the other teachers*, I noticed. We walked past the library, and then walked past the gym, which, while small, doubled as an auditorium. *God this lady walks fast.* And then, covered by shadows and arching walls, we saw it. A giant steel door. Room 445B. We opened the door and flipped on the harsh fluorescents. A thin patter of dust fell from the ceiling. I noticed the room was shaped like an octagon, and there were about 35 aged computers sitting on desks.

I felt a little claustrophobic. There was no window.

"What do you think?" Anne Marie asked.

"It appears to be a computer junkyard," I said.

Anne Marie smiled. "Yes, well the computers are a blessing. The kids can type all their papers up. But, I understand how you might want to get them out of here. Internet can be distracting." She wiped her fingers on top of a dusty table and then slapped her hands twice in the air. "Apparently the teacher who was in here before you had a few discipline problems."

"Oh yeah? The teacher before me?"

"Yes." She smiled nervously. "Now, not to disturb you or anything, Mr. Heffelapfle, but Mrs.Gunderez, as was her name, seemed to have some problems, a breakdown of sorts, midway through the second semester."

"Problems? Of what caliber?"

Anne Marie began to hook a computer up to one of the printers, but it wasn't working. The white knob wouldn't screw in. Suddenly, she became rather irate. "Fuck!"

And then, seeing as I was watching, apologized. "I'm sorry, it's just, all these memories."

She stared at me, perhaps to see if I would judge her. When I didn't, she continued.

"What Mrs. Gunderez had, actually, Mr. Heffelapfle, was called Intermittent Explosive Syndrome, or IES. It's a disease that affects approximately five percent of the population."

I stared at the broken computer parts. There were white knobs and cords strewn everywhere.

"Caused by high stress levels, the subject afflicted with the disease experiences total to partial loss of reasoning faculties - and then, over a period of time - explodes in a violent rage."

I smiled a false, reassuring grin. "Well, that's too bad. But I can assure you, Mrs. Fiehr - that will never happen to me."

"That's good, Leo. Because these kids...," she shook her head, "can be rough. And if a person is locked up in a room for eight hours a day, under mental duress, things can get a tad *taxing*, shall we say."

I was still grinning. That shit-eating grin. "But that's why I exercise every day, Mrs. Fiehr. We actually have a workout room at my apartment."

"Well that's good," she said. "Because in IES, the afflicted person destroys everything around them in a way that can lead to the destruction of school property. And sometimes, if but rarely, the syndrome can lead to the loss of innocent lives, which, unfortunately, is what happened in her case."

When I went home to my new apartment that night, I escaped the heat by sitting in the swimming pool. I shook my hair out and blew my nose. *This is heaven.* I gave Ed a call, but he didn't pick up. I stared at the palm trees. Now all I needed was a girlfriend. No use having a waterfall and being alone.

I decided I would drive around the city and try to meet an interesting woman in a coffee shop. Unfortunately, I quickly found out that Vegas isn't like normal cities. There aren't any coffee shops anywhere. There are only Starbucks, and there's no one in there but street people and losers.

I knew there were interesting people in Vegas. I just had to find them.

8.29.06

My alarm clock went off at 5:00 a.m. I was a little wearied, but it was the good kind of weary, ("healthy stress"). So I got up, jogged for half an hour, and then went over my positive affirmations while playing my Dr. Phil audiocassettes.

Cut past the crap, he said to me over my cassette player. *You are an amazing person who can be doing much more than you are doing.*

By golly, he was right, I thought.

You see, I didn't see myself as a teacher, per se. I'm not a teacher. I'm a *musician* having to pay *rent* having to be a *teacher,* forced to fit into this society, I thought. This of course meant finding a job, and working as a teacher was better than working at McFucko's.

So this seemed like a pretty good avenue to take while I climbed the ladder of success.

"SO DON'T FORGET!" I screamed into the mirror. I jumped up and down on my mini-trampoline while watching my ROCKY IV dvd. "I'm not a 'teacher', I'm a MUSICIAN! I'm not a 'teacher', I'm a MUSICIAN!"

I could hear my roommate in the living room letting out a groan.

"Fuck him," I said into the mirror, pounding down some Fiber All. "Don't forget who you really are, Bob Dylan Steven Spielberg George Lucas Indiana Jones Axle Rose."

I visualized myself playing guitar in front of millions of screaming girls. When one of them jumped on stage, I kicked her in the face.

"I'm a robot, oh God no," I said, pouring more cereal. "A cog in a wheel."

I remembered the famous words of Tom Petty: "I would have failed if I didn't have someone come along and show me the correct path."

Where is my someone? I looked in the closet. Not here. I looked under my bed. Not here either.

I don't get one. I don't get a special someone.

I put on my shirt and tie.

Wiped away a tear.

The new black slacks, where are they? *I have a Master's degree.* I have only one pair I'm going to be wearing the same fucking pair of black slacks everyday. *I'm a broke teacher.* No. It doesn't matter. Soon I'm going to be rich.

Fifty thousand dollars.

I used an extra scoop of super-control hair gel.

When I arrived at my room, Anne Marie, i.e., Mrs. FEAR explained to me the Order of Things.

"Okay, when the students get here," she said, huddling over, "we wait for them together, out here by this purple pole. Then you just make the students line up. I'll let my students go inside first, and then yours can go in. Are there any questions?"

"No. Sounds good."

We watched as a man with a long gray ponytail jogged over to us.

"Who's that?" I asked her.

He almost tripped over his own feet, and I could tell by the way he clapped his hands that he appeared to be subservient to someone.

"Leo, this is my husband."

I stared at him as he wiped off the excessive amount of tobacco spit that leaked between his lips and onto his beard.

"What grade are you teaching, Mr. Heffel?" he asked.

"8th-graders," I said.

His jaw clicked. It actually clicked. "Well ..." He shook my hand and just about broke it off. "We need people like you."

And before I could answer, he said, "Here they come."

Chapter 3
DAY ONE

"Please line up in a straight line," I said. "If you are in room 445B. Kids for room 445B please line up in a straight line and stare straight ahead. If you are in 445B line up here at this edge behind the purple pole."

As the kids walked past me, I shook their hands. "Good morning I'm happy to see you made it I've been preparing all summer for you good morning I'm happy good morning good I've been."

I went inside the classroom. There they were.

Holy crap I'm a teacher.

"Please take out your schedules and place them in front of you," I read from the script in my hand. It said: *Verify student's legal name and student number on the attendance roster.*

"Hey Mister," I heard someone say.

Place the student's legal name and student number on the roster sheet.

"Hey Mister," I heard someone say again.

"Please raise your hand, Lancelot," I said, continuing to read off my script. *Initial the student's schedule next to the period one and place an "E" on my temporary roster for the entry date.*

"Hey Mister. What's that silver thing in the middle of the floor?"

"Huh?"

I only caught a glimpse of it, a small silver package, tossed into the center of the floor by someone. And before I could say anything, there was a white light that blinded my eyes before sending out a rabid poisonous gas.

BANG!

It actually sounded like a gun going off. I dropped my script and hit the floor. I checked my body parts to see if any limbs had been blown off by shrapnel.

"WHAT WAS THAT?" I yelled. "WHO DID THAT? WHAT'S THAT SMELL?"

It smelled like a thousand farts had just been released.

"WHAT THE FUCK WAS THAT?"

The kids were coughing. "OUT!" I yelled.

"WE GOT SOME KIND OF BOMB," I yelled into the speaker pressing the white button.

"WHAT?" went the secretary from the other end of the line.

"...BOMB ..." I coughed. "CAN'T ...BREATHE ... *HELP* ..."

The kids were rushing out of my class. I put my shirt over my mouth. *What was that fucking chemical? Anthrax? Fuck! I breathed it in! And if it's not a chemical ... I don't want to have an allergic reaction!*

I ran outside.

The school police car pulled up, screeching its tires in front of my class, red lights and siren blaring.

I looked toward the office. The principal and secretary were running toward my class. Kids were bent over, coughing. Others were calling home and crying to their parents. Some were lying out on the grass, and taking in the sun. Others were just vomiting.

"GET BACK HERE!" I yelled at Luis and Michael who were running away.

"What's the situation?" someone said. It was the vice principal, Patricia.

"Some kind of fart bomb, released during class before I could take roll it was silver and it expanded..."

A police officer was taking notes on a pad from one of my students. Lancelot Jefferson. Black kid. Clean cut. Star basketball player.

"I don't know who threw it, shit," Lancelot said. "Ice Cream Man sells 'em for a quarter a piece."

"And who is this Ice Cream Man?" the cop asked.

"Drives in his truck," Lancelot said. "Ten stink bombs for three dollars."

I was suddenly really mad at that Ice Cream Man.

"Er, write down a description of the vehicle," the cop said.

"It's ice cream, man!" Lancelot said, getting mad. "Get away from me! Stop talking to me!"

"Who did it?"

"I'm not telling who did it! I'm not a narc!"

The bell rang. It was time for my second class of the day. I glanced at my watch. 9:00 a.m. There are five more periods in the day.

"Please line up in a straight line if you are in Room 445B if you are in Room 445B okay go inside sure oops you stepped on my shoe good to see you ha ha spit out your gum well okay you don't have to hello hi ha ha I'm Mr. Heffelapfle thanks for coming."

Holy crap I'm a teacher.

"Don't mind the smell," I announced, going into the class. "I kind of like it. Gosh, you guys look swell."

"FUCK YOU!" I heard someone say from the back of the room.

And then the battery came flying toward my head.

I actually dodged it, and everything went all slow motion for a second before I jumped back up, clapping. "Ha ha, good one guys. Unfortunately, I'm going to have to send you out of the room for that."

"Get out of my face teacher or I'll stab you!" some kid said.

"Nice to meet you," I said, looking at my roster. "Angelo. Please take your seat …"

"Make blood run down your shirt onto the floor!"

"Well," I said, smiling. "You shouldn't talk to teachers like that."

After I sent the kid out, I got a call from Patricia. She met me out in the hall.

"Listen, Mr. Heffelapfle. Do you see that line?"

She pointed towards the office. There was a line of eighth graders stretching out into the cafeteria, like you see at the opening of *Lord of the Rings*.

"That's the line to the Dean's office. There are so many kids in trouble here that we can't keep up with them."

"Okay."

"So I don't want you sending kids out of your room."

"But they threw a battery at me."

"You don't send a kid out of your room unless there is blood running down the aisles and into the hallway."

Blue jeans and tee-shirts, glued down, spiked up hair, (as if by rubber cement) - they looked pretty cool. But it suddenly occurred to me that these seemed to be the kind of kids who might come back years later to mess with their teacher. *I should probably be nice to them.*

No, don't approach it this way.

They might somehow smell my fear. It's funny, we didn't have kids like these back home in Montana. These kids were *big*. Like monster seniors in high school. NFL football players.

"You guys are big," I said, filling out some paperwork. I looked up. "Okay. This year we'll be studying sentence fragments, noun forms and the like. Do you guys understand?"

No one answered. "¿Hablas inglés?" I still hadn't realized that most of them couldn't speak English.

I looked at the two students to the left of me. I found them on my roster. Miguel and Jenny. *What were they doing under the table?* Were they dating? Just ignore it, I thought. *Can't save everyone.* It's time to teach. *Teach, man.*

I heard digging from behind me, over at my desk. I turned around. Once again, identified the kid on my roster. His name was Eddie. Number 188. *And he is rifling through my desk.*

"Can I help you Eddie?" I asked. Maybe I could just scare him away with the tone of my voice. *"Eddie."*

But before I could continue, I heard this bizarre, witch-like cackle. That's right - a cackle. I looked in the center of the classroom. Number 331. Linda Trejo.

And the second time I saw one of those batteries coming at my head, I heard her insane cackle, her tongue hanging down, all long and dangly, violently shaking her head back and forth.

"Lyar!" she roared.

"Excuse me?" I said.

"RAAAR!"

"What? Okay Linda – thank you for that." I took a sip from my coffee. "We'll need to work on your pronunciation of some of these syllables, because sometimes it's a little hard to hear what you're ..."

And in the middle of all this, I'm approached by Miriam Lopez. She's this darling girl, really, with darling glasses, and darling gum in her mouth, who starts telling me about how the door that's in the corner of my room, kind of hidden in the corner of my room there, leads to upstairs.

"Sit down," I said. "It doesn't mean I don't like you. But Mr. Heffelapfle's busy right now."

"And it is upstairs, at the top of the building," she said, "where the old woman died in the swimming pool years ago."

The teacher before me?

"I can't hear what you're saying," I said. "Eddie get out from behind my things. Linda, stop making those grunting noises!"

A paper airplane flew across the room.

"Can we go in that door?"

"LYARRR!"

"I'm going to stab you Mister."

"Stop saying that Angelo."

I looked at it. Just an ordinary door. Hm. It *is* strange. Has it been here this whole time? *A door has appeared out of nowhere. Ha ha, no. Get real. You just didn't notice it.*

"No, we can't go in the door," I said.

"WHY NOT???" Miriam shouted.

"Don't yell."

"WHY NOT?"

"Because. Sit down. Eddie get out of my desk."

"Do you have a key for it?" she continued.

"No," I said.

I felt the key in my pocket.

Man that coffee was kicking in. I was starting to sweat a little. "No. Sit down. Do you want me to call the principal?"

"Can we go up there?"

"If you're good maybe one day," I said. I looked over at Linda. *"Lyyaaar."*

Chapter 4

THE FAT CAT

Okay, we get three minutes in between classes. I jogged down the gym track to the restroom, but some guy in a bright red workout suit blocked my path. I slowed down. "Excuse me," I said. "Bathroom."

"Mr. Heffelapfle? Hi! It's me, Gary Schendel!"

I stopped my jog and took a deep breath. This was a big guy.

"You probably don't remember me, Mr. Heffelapfle," he said, "because that first day was such a blur. But you and me, we met in teacher orientation."

He had on one of those wrinkle-less shirts that made his skin look plastic. He breathed heavily, had a big beard, and a lot on his mind.

He scratched his chin. Played with his nose hair.

"You know, Leo," he said, really spelling out the diction. "The Art of Teaching is a book that always changes, from student to student, year to year."

I massaged my dick. I appeared to have a constant need to urinate.

"And back in the olden days," he said, "the teacher in America was respected."

He reached into a duffel bag. His hand searched for a moment, and when he found what he was looking for, he smiled before pulling it out. It was a plank of plywood, coated in primer. There was a rusty nail sticking out from the corner.

He licked his lips. His eyes were aflame.

"Woodrow Wilson once said, *'Talk softly and carry a big stick.'* Do you have a big stick, Mr. Heffelapfle?"

"No," I said.

"You want this one?"

I shook my head.

"You might need it."

I gave him a conciliatory smile.

"Okay, well come back to me if you change your mind."

He put the stick back in his bag and smiled as though he had just shared with me some great secret that I could use in my classroom.

"Okay guys! Sit down!" I said to my next class.

These guys were a lot better.

"Sit down. Take out a pen and a notebook. Put your backpacks underneath your tables. If you don't have your journal notebook, considering it is the first day of school, take out a single piece of paper and answer the question on the board: *Do I like being indoors or outdoors more often?*"

I began to take roll.

"I like being outdoors," I said, as I'm doing this. "Because where I'm from, there's wildlife. Trees and deer that roam through your backyards. I like to play my guitar for them."

It was about this time in my first period that the bomb went off. And about this time in my second period that the battery came at my head. *So just hurry.* It only takes one minute to take roll, but in one second we can have a fatal accident.

"Okay guys!" I said. "We have got to get in to the wonderful world of vocabulary! So GET UP, stand up, and SHAKE out your bodies! Come on! Stand up! SHAKE SHAKE SHAKE!"

"YEAAAAH!" Little Matthew screamed, punching his fists in the air. (Why do some kids get named 'Little'? I don't know. He just looked like a little baby. A little goochy. A goochy woochy goo goo.)

"That's good!" I said. "Good!"

You can't do this with other age groups. They wouldn't have the energy. They would be looking at me, apathetic in their seats. But eighth graders?

"YEAAA!" someone else yelled, as a desk got pushed over.

Another one was launched into the wall.

The class is actually standing up, I thought. *This is a lot of fun. I can handle this.* The bookcase in the corner fell over, throwing dictionaries everywhere, but I didn't care because we were going to have a good time learning today.

"STAND UP AND SHAKE OUT YOUR BODIES!"

I saw the boys in front were really getting into it. But there were a group of girls in back who apparently refused to participate.

"GIRLS!" I said. "JUMP UP WITH US!"

They ignored me and kept on talking among themselves. *I can't stand this*, I thought. *This is annoying. I don't want their apathy to spread like some vile fungus.*

"GIRLS! Get up and dance with us!"

And then I heard their first piece of advice. "Shut up you fruity freak."

I stopped dancing.

"Who said that?"

The girls pulled their desks apart so that I could see the single largest 13-year-old girl on the planet.

"I did, bitch," she said.

She threw her wrapper on my floor.

"And who might you be?" I asked.

"None of your damn fuckin' business," she said. "Look at the size of your forehead. Takes up the whole entire room."

I looked on my roster. #2543. Ramona Gomez. Eating cookies. Throwing wrappers on my floor. Belching like some vile pig.

"That's it," I said. "I don't know who you are. But you're not going to stay here very long. You're out of here."

I sauntered over to the button on the wall.

"You're out of here."

A little note about the button: I didn't want to use it too much. The button is only supposed to be pressed in emergencies. And this was nothing. I wondered if Ramona knew this. To test my theorem, I pretended to press the button, only to find something amazing occurred.

"NO! NO! NO, MISTER! Please, I'm sorry! I swear I won't do it again!"

I pretended to press the button again.

"NO! NO! NO, MISTER! PLEASE! I'm SORRY! Can I clean up your desk for you?" she said, begging. Like a dog. A Pavlov's dog.

I just stared at her. I pretended to press the button again.

"NO NO NO MISTER! PLEASE! I'M SORRY! I SWEAR!"

You don't need a big stick, I thought. You just need a big button.

I soon discovered that the button only worked for certain kids.

I had a study hall, in which Angelo and Hashim came back to my class, and instead of studying quietly and playing chess, they decided it was best to take off their pants.

"This is not how eighth graders act," I said. "There's something wrong with you!"

I watched Hashim. He watched me back. These wide eyes.

"So I'm pressing the white button, Hashim, so you can further yourself in the beginning of what I think will be a transformation for you. However, some people never get out of psychological counseling."

"If you do that, I'm going to stab you FUCKER!" Angelo barked.

I stared at him.

"Just joking," Angelo said. "Ha ha. Please don't press the button, mister."

"Sorry," I said. "It's too late for you. Goodbye."

I pressed the button.

No answer.

"Goodbye," I repeated, pressing it again.

No answer.

Angelo and Hashim looked at one another and smiled.

"They don't like you!" Angelo roared.

Hashim kicked his chair over. "Now I'm going to ROCK OUT!"

"ANGELO SIT DOWN!"

I pressed the button, kids were screaming, papers were flying, fists were flying, a cruise missile flew across the room, and that Linda Ruinowski from second period mysteriously showed up again "LYAAR! LYAAR!"

And then, somewhere in this god-awful mess, the door to my room flung open. Everything kind of went in slow motion. We all quickly became silent, and looked at each other and then at the door. *No, not the principal!*

We all stared.

Everyone shut their mouths.

The door swung softly to a halt.

My eyes scanned for problem kids, quickly, then I looked back at the door. I scratched my nose, yawned softly, to pretend as though I had it all under control.

And then - this short, bald, middle aged Latino jumped into the room, and all the kids yelled, "CAPTAIN AMERICA!"

He thrust his hip to the side and said to me, "I'm the hall monitor and I could hear your kids all the way out in the hall. What seems to be the problem, Mr. H?"

"These guys," I said.

I pointed at Angelo and Hashim.

The two boys looked at each other, and, sensing future detentions, shouted "RUN!" Captain America tried to catch them, but they broke his grip and escaped out the door.

The two of us just stared at each other.

"So what are you doing Saturday?" he asked.

"Oh, I don't know."

"Why don't you come to church with me and the girlfriend?"

"Huh? Yeah, sure."

"It's really cool." He handed me a brochure.

There was a picture of a lion with wings on it.

"Well I had been thinking about it, actually," I said. "I feel kind of lost."

Chapter 5

THE PERFECT STUDENT

I was really looking forward to the last period of the day, because this was the famed accelerated class. It would be really nice to have some students who I could train and mold into future Leo's. I got some Discover magazines especially for this group. Maybe we could talk about black holes and poisonous spiders. *If I can just affect ONE person*, I thought. *This kid could become the next Oprah.*

Every period Mrs. Fiehr and I stood out by the purple pole. Her kids were really well behaved. But they were wimpy sixth graders. Eighth graders are 10 times larger. They turn from chimps into apes by that time.

"Mr. Heffelnaple," she said, "I want to introduce you to someone."

I looked up.

"Your future star, Leo. This is Maria."

Standing before me was this gorgeous muchacha who had large maple eyes and shoulder length brown hair. Her beauty intensified when she saw me. And while none of these kids looked liked eighth graders, she *really* didn't. *Was it the hormones in the meat? Was it the radioactive water? Why, do Latinos age faster? Is this true? I don't know. I'm from Montana.* She stuck out her hand to shake mine.

"I'm Maria."

"Oh. Hi."

"You'll have to excuse Mr. Heffelape," Anne Marie explained. "He's had a rough first day. Someone lit a bomb off in his class."

Maria was staring at me strangely. "How old are you, Mister?"

But before I could answer, the bell rang, so we had to go inside the class. Maria held the door open for me.

"Uh, thanks."

Once inside, I noticed that my roll book had gotten knocked to the ground. There were papers and pencils all over the place. I bent over to pick them up. Before I could finish, my ears were filled with a most disturbing sound.

"Whoooo-hooo!"

I looked up.

It was the girls! Making whoo sounds!

"Tell me you didn't just whoo at me," I said.

Maria was looking at me.

"Don't whoo," I said, shaking my head.

As I bent down to pick up the pencils, again, I heard the construction workers whistling.

"Wooo-wheee!"

I played along. Flexed my biceps. "That's right," I said. "I'm a good looking guy."

But then I saw one little girl looking at me like I was a pedophile. I quickly changed my tune.

"But you can't whoo and whistle at me like I belong in a magazine, even if I do," I said.

I sat down at my desk.

Again the girls went crazy.

On one hand this was funny, but on the other, I couldn't have the principal walk in and see this, so I started to get a little nervous. I reverted back to my Master's degree training, and said the first thing that came to my mind.

"Don't," I said, like a little girl.

"Don't what, Mister?" Maria asked.

I sucked in my gut. "Don't."

But before I could continue, Maria had climbed on top of the table. Apparently this would be a good time to start taking off her clothes, she must have thought. Because that's what she was doing.

"HE CAN'T CONTROL US! LET'S GET CRAZY!" she shouted, gyrating her hips.

Holy crap. I'm a teach ...

Everyone was shouting, and it was at this moment I was introduced to Chad, who I will from here on out call 'The Rocket,' because he was blasting himself into the side of my filing cabinet with his head.

Oh my God.

"Everybody stop!" I said. My eyes began to water. I was almost too tired to get control. A migraine was kicking in. *Where's my coffee? Did I put it over here?* I thought. *I need my coffee - .*

Someone had turned the music on. My lights were blinking on and off like a rave.

"SIT DOWN!" I screamed. "WHAT'S WRONG WITH YOU?"

They all stopped, and looked over at Maria to see what she would say.

Again, she looked at me strangely. Sizing me up. Like I was a piece of chicken. She buttoned her shirt back together.

"Yes," she said, finally, as if to agree with me. "Sit down everybody."

When they heard her, they took to their seats.

I looked at her, angrily. "Don't do that."

"Don't," she said, imitating me. Then she tilted her hand at the wrist. "*Don't.*"

After the last bell of the day, I felt like nuclear shit. I walked into Anne Marie's room stuck in some somnambulating state. She was writing Latin roots on the blackboard. She had flashcards out on the tables to memorize new students' names.

"So how was the star student?" she asked, smiling but not looking at me.

"Who's that?" I asked. I grabbed a sponge from her wash bin and squeezed it. "Oh you mean Maria? She's good…"

"Oh yeah. She's terrific."

The air in her room had that harsh smell of cleaning chemicals. My eyes began to blink. *Is there chlorine leaking in here?*

"She's like a daughter to me," she said. "I had her for years. She was great."

"Huh."

I was doing everything I could to not start coughing. I had read somewhere that janitors who use cleaning supplies suffer from brain damage over a period of time.

"How long have you been teaching?" I asked.

"As long as I've been cleaning these tables," she said. "Some 30 years."

"Huh."

She smelled her fingers. "And Maria is one of the best I've seen. In fact …"

I thought of the star student up on the table asking students if they wanted a lap dance.

"…you can even leave the room and have her run the class for you. She's *terrific.*"

"Huh? What?" I asked.

"Oh yeah," Anne Marie said. "I would have no problem doing that."

I scratched my chin. "Really?"

Is this just me? I *have* never taught before, I thought. I obviously have no idea what I'm doing. Maybe I was a little too hard on her. Maybe I need to reexamine this. Maybe I … maybe I'm stupid. I threw the sponge on the table.

"Maria really is …" she said, beneath moist blue eyes, "the daughter I never had."

I went home, questioning life. Okay, I need to really focus on these lesson plans. If I don't, then every year after this won't run smoothly. This will just take a few hours a night. If they're to be good, that is. You don't want to just give the kids vocabulary worksheets. I remembered those teachers.

But what about your music?

I know, I know.

I'll just put it aside, just for a little bit.

I sat out in the Jacuzzi.

Chapter 6

POST TRAUMATIC MARIA
SYNDROME

9.1.06

Because I wouldn't allow Maria to perform strip shows, she decided to get even with me.

"Eww, what stinks," she said, every time I walked by.

Or was she just being really honest?

Either way, this could not continue.

"Maria, stop it," I said.

As I walked about the room, checking students' papers, I thought, *Jesus, what if it IS me?* I covertly smelled my armpits by trying to pretend to scratch my elbow with my chin. Some kids noticed this. I continued to walk, pace the room.

Do I avoid her desk, now, so that she will stop saying this? I smell fine. You smell fine. And I did. I smelled fine. At least my armpits did. *But what about my ass?*

You stayed up late last night, playing music. But you still had time to take a shower. Or did you?

Maria sits at crotch-level. *That was a hell of a shit I took earlier this morning. Dammit Ed. Fucking Fiber All spraying in the stall.* "You will need a fire hose to clean your ass out," I remember Ed saying. "It *rakes* your system."

"Eww, Mister," she said again, as I came within five feet of her. Her voice was *so* loud. Everyone was beginning to take notice.

Oh no, will you just shut up, kid?

"The smell is only around when you're around," Maria's best friend, Lacey, now jumped in.

My heart started to pick up again. *They're lying. No. It's not me.*

"Yes it appears to be some kind of cologne," I said, sniffing the air loudly.

"No, it's not a cologne," Maria said.

They made hand signals to one another that I could not decipher. Signals that included plugging their nose.

My thoughts then flashed to the encounter I had with Ed, driving my car down from Montana. "Would you please at least hang up a deodorizer? You know, strong smells like this can transfer into your clothing."

Oh my god. I had to get to a bathroom and wash myself as fast as I could, because what if it *was* me? I am not *beyond* being a smelly male.

I quickly went over to the phone in the corner and pretended to call one of my fellow teachers.

"Why hello, Mister Z, thank you for calling earlier. This is unexpected. Oh yes, ha ha. You want those file folders? Of course. Yes, I'll send a student over with them, immediately. Actually, they have some private things in them. I had better bring them over myself."

I could feel all eyes on me.

I walked over to the file cabinet and pretended to grab some high class government documents. Once in hand, I then walked out of the classroom. "I'll be back. Hold the fort for me, Maria."

As soon as I hit the hallway, the sprint began.

Kids' lockers sprang past me in geometric patterns. *Where are the fuckin' firehoses?* I damn near hit Patricia in the doorway ("*Why do they make the doors like this?*" "*Why don't you slow down?*") before I finally found the bathroom and hosed myself down. But I had to be CAREFUL not to get any water on my shirt, otherwise they could tell. They could TELL that Maria had *intimidated* me. *Intimidated* me enough to make me make up this weird story about file folders. Intimidated me enough to make me run down the hallway, so everybody's thinking I'm *shitting fire*. Intimidated me enough to go into the restroom and shove my head into the toilet. Intimidated me enough to damn near have a heart attack.

Within 30 seconds, I walked back into the classroom. My armpits and crotch were wet. Beads of sweat. I can only imagine the discussion while I was gone. "He ran off to take a bath."

"Yeah, well have you seen my *car*?" I wanted to say. "This is *nothing*. That strange odor you are picking up is from the piss bottles I use to pee in while driving on my way to work."

They would stare at me, in disbelief. But instead of stopping I would continue, and mar them for life. "My ex-girlfriend used to like to be peed on. She was one sick chick. But that's what they don't tell you, about life. But I'm your teacher, so I consider it my responsibility. Any questions?"

I walked up to the front of the room to make an announcement. "Excuse me, kids. Quiet, please."

"Ewww, Mister."

Maria. What was wrong with her?

I turned to her. She was waving her hand in front of her nose.

"Maria," I said. "Knock it off young lady."

She looked at me, innocently. "Knock what off?"

Blink, blink.

"Insinuating that I *smell*," I said. "Which I don't. I know I don't. Not anymore."

I just took a shower.

"I *know* I don't," I said, standing closer to her, now, in full confidence.

"It didn't smell and now it does," Lacey said. "Strangely enough, right when you walked in, sir."

I glared at The Imitator. "If you don't knock it off, I'm going to send you down to the counselor to have your nose examined."

"Knock *what* off?" Maria bounced back. "MISTER! YOU'RE ALWAYS PICKING ON ME!"

"No I'm not," I said. "Just because I won't let you do your little nudie acts. So be quiet. If you continue to talk I will send you away. Far away."

"I WANT TO GO TO THE COUNSELOR'S!"

"Well that's where I'm sending you," I said.

"*I want to call my mom,*" Maria said.

"So do I," I said.

I twitched my nose. "What *is* that smell?"

I looked over at The Rocket. He seemed tired from all that sweating he probably built up in gym class.

"It's your *room*, Mister."

"Well," I grunted, "I have to put up with smells all day, Maria. And let's pretend that it *was* me. I smell *you* and your little buddies all day. I am immersed in every type of fungus known to man. I can't keep plants in my room because they wilt and die. I can't have a girlfriend because smelly kids are on my clothes."

"*Don't blame that on us, Mister. That's YOUR fault.*"

"No it's not," I said, and then made a chopping motion on my neck. "Go to the counselor. Tell her about why I can't have a girlfriend."

"You're always blaming me, Mister," Maria said.

This was becoming exasperating.

Regardless, I played along.

"No I'm not," I said. "You're always blaming ME. The smell was *not* me, I'm practically certain of it. *But even if it was*, which it wasn't, you shouldn't try to nail me, to humiliate me in front of the class and then to continue to talk after I ask you to stop."

"I never said it was you," Maria said.

And I thought about it, and she was right. She never *did* say it was me. Huh.

I looked at the girls.

Huh.

Besides, Maria did use a *yellow* highlighter.

That's gotta mean something.

Most of the kids didn't even bring pencils or papers to class.

Lacey looked up at me. Blink blink. "We were just joking, Mister."

"Well," I said. "I'm not joking."

"We were just joking," Maria said.

"Well." I breathed deeply. *Who did Maria remind me of?* She seemed so sweet, so tender all of a sudden. "Well, so was I. About all that counselor malarkey. You may continue working on your test."

Maria looked at Lacey, and they both continued working.

9.7.06

Sometimes before class there was no time to run down the hallway to go to the restroom. So I would go over to my door, lock it, and then kneel behind my desk, where I kept the extra water bottles.

It was quite a brewery between my desk and the car. I filled them up, one at a time, only spilling a little bit here and there. And then, when I was done, I placed them gently back into the desk drawers, to be picked up at a later date (a date which as of this point is yet to be determined).

I hummed to Willie Nelson's hit "To All the Women I've Loved Before", and smiled, realizing that all teachers, particularly males, secretly pee in bottles.

9.8.06

"So now she hates me," I said.

The counselor placed her hands together. Mrs. Lovely. Always overloaded with students. "It switches back and forth. This week they hate you, next week they love you, Mr. Hefrfreffel."

"Right. All the same," I said, "she shouldn't hate me. I like her."

Maria reminded me of some old third grade girlfriend I had. A little girl named Kim Johnson who somehow affected my entire life. And you know what they say, when you have hard times, you regress back to those first pivotal relationships in your life and play them like a record in your mind, over and over.

Kim Johnson was the hottest girl in the class. I know it's hard to imagine, especially because we're dealing with the mind of third graders. But the bottom line is that she kissed me while walking to class one day. Which was great, until she kissed another boy – Jair Springfield. And then she kissed David Ryman on some kissing frenzy, unable to stop herself, like she was going crazy.

I sat in my bedroom at the time, playing Olivia Newton John records, crying with tears that just sprang out of nowhere because I realized that my life was moving too fast.

"I'm only in the third grade!" I remember thinking, staring at the bubbles in my bathtub. "She's got to go. Kim's got to go."

So I dumped her and regretted it for the rest of my life.

I'll never forget her looking at me with those eternal blue eyes. *"Don't leave me. I love you. I love you, Leo."*

Kim would later become the most popular girl in high school and become the prom queen, coveted by all men, that sort of thing, while I was stuck in the library with the other nerd-lings reading about poisonous spiders.

Suddenly, I realized that I was still in Mrs. Lovely's office. I had been spacing out the entire time.

She stared back at me, expressionless.

9.20.06

And so my knee is a shattered waffle cone. Fucking yoga after work. What a joke. *What was I thinking? Good for the body? Good place to meet girls? Good way to clear my mind? I should have stuck to Starbucks!*

My biggest mistake was coming home after school and getting all stupidly spiritual. I guess I needed to "relax" after getting my ass pounded into submission by insubordinate Maria.

9.21.06

La niña.

Hates me and then loves me.

Every day with her is a strip show or trying to insinuate that I smell. Just try to imagine weeks upon weeks of this. And then you just start ignoring her, you have no choice. And then she comes up with the perfect comeback to get your attention.

Like today which was another day of hell. I wrote her up for climbing under the desks. And she made me pay for it, as usual. And what's *my* problem? I don't condemn her. I act like her delinquent behavior just rolls off my shoulders because, on some level, she's not Maria. She's *Kim*. My subconscious is afraid that if I mess this up, then I won't become Prom King.

We play a reading game called "Popcorn." Here's how it goes: If a student says, "Popcorn Josh," as an example, then that means it is Josh's turn to read. After Josh is done reading, then he calls out "Popcorn Matthew."

Now Matthew was this totally adorable Asian kid, who had never spoken more than two words at a time in his entire life. His notebooks were filled with drawings of Stinky Cheese Man and characters out of XBOX.

"Popcorn Matthew," someone said.

So here was Matthew, reading away. I thought he was reading at least, because his mouth was moving, although nothing was coming out.

So I said, "Hey Matthew, read louder. If you don't, I'm going to give you detention. A little logic lesson. How's that sound?"

Matthew's eyes opened as wide as possible.

"If you don't do x, you get y."

Before I could say 'I'm joking' I was interrupted.

"YOU CAN'T DO THAT!" I hear from the back of the room. Maria.

What a horrible, ghastly scream.

"YOU CAN'T DO THAT!"

It hurts my ears.

"I'M GOING TO WRITE YOU UP AND BRING YOU TO THE DEAN'S!" she says.

Her eyes are really on fire.

"I said I was …" I begin.

Josh, one of her peons, really enjoys this. She probably kissed him on the cheek between classes.

"Yeah Mister, we're going to get you FIRED," he says. "Yeaaah."

Suddenly, out of nowhere, as if rehearsed, the students begin to clap and stomp in total unison - BOOM-BOOM-CHUCK…BOOM-BOOM-CHUCK - to "We Will Rock You." The Rocket springs off one of the side desks. Papers go flying everywhere. Little Alberto has O'Brian's rope and is doing jumping jacks while somebody else is taking a leak in the corner.

"Send me to the DEAN'S to get FIRED?" I say to Maria, over the ruckus. "So *that's* your loyalty to me? SO I MADE A WRONG WORD CHOICE, I MADE A MISTAKE IT'S THE END OF THE DAY - I'M TIRED!"

Someone was rolling in an old Civil War cannon, and pointing it at my desk.

"I DON'T CARE," Maria shouts.

"BUT I DO have a point! Matthew's got to read loud enough to be heard!"

"WHAT? I CAN'T HEAR YOU!"

"MATTHEW'S GOT TO READ LOUD ENOUGH TO BE HEARD!"

"WHAT?"

"HOW IS HE SUPPOSED TO GET A JOB?"

All the kids are screaming.

Little Josh is backing her up. "SHOULD we go to the Dean's? SHOULD WE GO TO THE DEAN'S?" he says, as if to dare her, completely oblivious of me.

And then the air in the room seemed to still. It was like we were on a perfect blue lake, and there was Kim, I mean, Maria, staring at me, all grown up, wearing some flamenco dress. *You'll never have me*, say her eyes.

I look at Maria.

She glares back.

"I'M SORRY," I screech into the heavens. "I'M SORRY!"

And then, I just start confessing everything. "I should have never dumped Kim back in the third grade – because now look, it appears as though her phantom has returned in the soul of this child! That's right! That's who you remind me of! (But we don't need to get into that –)."

At this, Maria took a deep breath of air, and clenched her hand like a music director telling the band to stop playing. Suddenly everybody stopped. The Rocket went back to his desk. O'Brian put away the jump rope. The lights came back on. The rave music stopped.

"Popcorn Cynthia," she said. "You may progress where little Matthew stopped."

And the game continued.

9.26.06

I never really understood what stress was until la niña entered my life. I would go home at the end of the night and literally not be able to get her image to stop vertigo-ing in my head.

I felt like I had been hijacked on some airplane.

So I called up Ed, who was somewhere in Iraq. Our long talks helped me to get through the situations, and who knows, maybe she'd make a good character in a book one day.

"You ever seen the Omen?" I said, floating in the swimming pool. "God if this girl has this kind of affect on me, I can't imagine the future terror she'll put her future boyfriends through. I'm just her teacher, man. She'll definitely cause a suicide or two."

"That's too bad. How's the Fiber All?"

"Damn near shit myself in sixth period."

I could tell he liked to hear this.

"Well. Well then not all is lost."

9.28.06

Just to deal with the post traumatic stress that I incurred by having Maria in my class, I had to undergo sessions of hypnotherapy on audio cassette. If you're a teacher, I recommend, "Verbal Rape" by Charles Lloyd.

I also started praying, which really seemed to help. I simply knelt in a comfortable position on the floor, behind my desk, and prayed to a variety of Gods, just to make sure I got the right one. Fifteen minutes to Jesus, 15 minutes to Muhammed, and 15 to the Egyptian sun god Thoth.

"Please send someone to save me," I said.

Oh. And we never played "Popcorn" again.

Chapter 7
MY FIRST EVALUATION

9.29.06

After school, all the eighth grade teachers were supposed to meet in room 611 to discuss "departmental curriculum." The only two teachers who showed up were me and JC Fowler. JC was in her sixties, and she had a big red recliner in her room that she would sit in, eating potato chips and correcting papers. She was Black – the only Black teacher in our building. The other teachers were Caucasian or Latino, shipped in from small towns across the U.S.

When she saw me come in, she put on her tiny glasses that had those strings that go behind your head in case they fall off. I suddenly noticed, that like many of the other teachers, she was overweight, and her body impinged on her knees to the effect that she carried a cane.

Every inch of her classroom walls were covered with famous Black people, how-to-do cursive posters, and every item that you would expect from someone who had been teaching for 40 years.

"So where is everyone?" I asked.

"Meeting was cancelled. Didn't nobody tell you? Ah, well that's because you're all over by yourself, in The Hole."

"The Hole?"

"Yeah, that's what we call the room you're in." She began doing stretches as we spoke. "At least it's big. A big room. Look at how tiny my room is. I asked for a nice big room, but Patricia gave it to you."

"Patricia sure is nice."

"She ain't nice. She's only acting nice because you're new."

My eyelid fluttered. "What?"

"You heard me."

"But she's down there, in her office, working hard," I argued.

"Working hard? At what? How about watching the paint dry on the walls! Working hard, my ass. The only thing she works hard at is being a bitch and eating carpet, if you know what I mean."

"Oh."

She lowered her voice about 10 notches. "What you've got to do, Leo, is ally yourself with someone. Anyone."

"Ally myself?"

"Yes. So you don't get eaten alive. Where's that other newbie, Mr. Ryder? Yes, go buddy-buddy up to him, trade stories, stay under the sight of that bitch and her guns. He already went to the union on her ass."

"Well, okay. It was sure nice meeting you."

"Get out of my room."

"Okay. Bye."

"Bye Leo."

9.30.06

I remember my first evaluation.

I was so happy because when Patricia came inside my class, the kids were so good to me. They actually shut up. They pretended to be reading. They pretended to ask questions. And I actually read to them the first half of the class, which had never happened before.

Meanwhile, Patricia jotted notes on her little yellow notepad with her red marker.

This is the best class I have ever had, I thought. *I'm so lucky that Patricia came to observe me today.* I mean, she could have come in on a day when Hashim was having an ADHD episode, or when The Rocket was smashing his head into my file cabinet, or something like that.

The bell rang, and all the kids walked out quietly.

"You may be excused," I said. I took two huffs on my fingernails and cleaned them on my collar.

I looked up at Patricia, who had hung around. Apparently she wanted to give me some thoughts on my teaching. I was looking forward to this, because it was my best day.

"You know, I've seen a lot of teachers, Mr. Heffelapfle," she said. She rearranged her red markers one by one into a tiny little box. Then she looked up at me. "And either you have it or you don't. And you don't."

Every day after work my roommate Colin and I would meet up to talk about our new teaching jobs.

"So what happened at school today?" he asked.

I smashed a Healthy Ones TV dinner into the microwave and pushed the timer button as hard as I could.

"Huh? What? Oh, sorry," I said. "I was evaluated today."

He smiled. "How'd it go?"

I slammed one of the cabinet doors shut. Then I let out a long sigh of relief and even burst out laughing a little bit. I looked at him and smiled.

"I thought it went fine," I said. I raised my hands in the air in disbelief.

"What?" he asked.

"But Patricia says that I need to be like a million times stricter."

"Really?"

"Which makes no sense, because today when Patricia came into my class, all the kids were quietly reading from their books and following along."

"Really?"

"Yeah, I was like: *thank God she came in today. Good job, guys, makin' me look good.* And after she left I gave them candy between classes. *Just like we drilled, guys, so here's your reward. Neccos.* "

"That's fantastic."

While I ate my Healthy Ones, Colin opened up his new carton of cigarettes.

"Then she said..." I paused, actually unable to continue my sentence.

"What's wrong?"

"Nothing." I stared off. "Nothing. Then she called me down to her room."

"Mr. Heffelapfle, if you're on campus, please come down to the office."

I took a seat in front of the vice principal.

She handed me a paper to sign.

"You know, I'm just going to tell you now," she said. "I have ... very serious concerns ... very grave concerns ... over your discipline skills."

"What?" I answered, taking a bite out of my donut. "But the kids were sitting there, quietly reading."

She gave me a charitable smile. "That's what you thought, Mr. Heffelapfle. But every time you looked down in your book to read to them, the students were *throwing* things at each other, making faces, and making fun of you."

I took a deep gulp of air.

"Like you're an idiot," she said.

I didn't know how to respond.

I said, "But I thought they were doing so well."

"Well that's because *I* am there. They *know* me, so they get good. I have what is called *command presence*."

She handed me the form to sign. I noticed that I had been graded on a scale of one to 10. I had been given a one.

"One is the highest?" I asked.

"No," she said.

I walked out of her office, with my head hanging low. I slumped back into my class, only to face the wretched beasts.

"So what are your plans?" Colin asked, eyeing my Healthy Ones.

"New rules," I said, pulling out a pad and pen. "Tomorrow the kids are going to meet Sergeant Heffelapfle."

Chapter 8
SERGEANT HEFFELAPFLE

10.1.06

The writing on the board said:

The Number One Rule: If you get in trouble with Mr. Heffelapfle for any reason, *don't argue with him.* Just nod your head and say 'yes sir'. If you proceed to argue with Mr. Heffelapfle, he will take overwhelming action.

This will occur by:

1. Giving you a verbal command to stop.
2. Pressing the big white button for Captain America.
3. Calling up your parents, (which is very embarrassing).
4. Sending you to the Dean's for potential expulsion.
5. Sending you to Mrs. Fiehr's room, (her room makes my room look like paradise).
6. Please stop being bad because it's important to be good.

"Angelo!"

He had just thrown a DD battery at Spencer's head.

I love Spencer. He's the only kid I like. He has big glasses like I used to have.

Spencer had to leave and ran out of the room, moaning and applying pressure to the wound to try and make his face stop bleeding.

"Angelo!" I shrieked. "What does the Number One Rule say on the board?"

"Nuthin'," he said.

"*Read it to me*, Angelo, or *I'm sending you to the Dean's.*"

"Call his mom, Mister," Lancelot said

I looked at Lancelot. Then back at Angelo.

"Yeah. Or I'll call your mom," I said. "What does the the Number One Rule say?"

"It says 'you're a FAGGOT.'"

The class ostensibly enjoyed this kind of humor. I could tell by the way they screamed with laughter. Apparently Angelo was a future standup comedian.

"NO ANGELO!" I roared, standing above him in the light. "READ WHAT'S ON THE BOARD!"

He chuckled and looked up at the board.

"*Read it*," I said.

According to the internet, *command presence* is what drill sergeants in the Marines refer to as "respect by observation."

Ed set up a conference call direct from Iraq. Corporal Brian Madden explained to me, on Skype, just what it was that I lacked:

"Well, Mr. Heffelapfle, I noticed that none of the company gave the new drill Sergeants any respect. However, whenever I would walk into the room, everyone would instantly quiet down."

He pulled out a 10-inch carving knife. "Why does one guy have it and another, not? A lot of this respect has to do with the way one dresses. *It's where you get your clothes, Leo.*"

I looked down at Angelo, in my teacher pants.

He was so stupid and ... I was going to crush him ... yeah.

"READ IT!" I yelled, pointing at the board's instructions.

He chuckled under his breath. "The Nubber One Roll thing," he said, "if you get in trouble with … Mr. Fucking Dick Fuck …"

"Angelo!"

"…Donut…ar-gew."

"THAT'S CORRECT!" I said. "SEE HOW EASY THAT WAS."

"Yes Ma'am!"

Again, the class went crazy.

Either you have it or you don't.

My fists shook as I looked down at him.

And you don't.

I walked away, tensing my eyebrows. "Close enough," I said. Spencer came back in with a giant piece of gauze on his face.

"You okay, fella?" I asked. "Hey, look at me. Look at me. You okay, little guy?"

He didn't respond.

In all the commotion, I didn't notice that someone had stolen my Walkman. How they got it was a mystery, because I kept it inside a locked drawer. But that wasn't the scary part. The scary part was that *inside* the Walkman was a blank tape. But it wasn't really blank. On it was me singing in my car and talking about God knows what.

I liked to record myself here and there. Audio journals.

A segment of the tape apparently had me and Alexandria (ex-girlfriend, pee) on it. (I'm not going to get into it.)

I kept the tape as a memento. A souvenir of the good old days. Were we having sex on it? Or something worse? I couldn't remember. I just pressed record. I was always pressing record.

That blank tape, I thought, if placed in the wrong hands, could cause one hell of a scandal. I laughed, nervously. *It is kind of funny.*

But then I realized I could get fired. I *could.*

It wasn't funny anymore.

"*Oh Leo! Why are you recording us?*" I suddenly remembered Alexandria saying.

"Shut up," I said. "Just hold still ...you fucking ... bitch..."

Chapter 9

THE CASE OF THE MISSING
WALKMAN

10.2.06

The dictionary defines conniption as "a fit of hysteria or panic."
I was more on the panic end. At four in the morning I was just lying
there, playing my self-confidence tapes which weren't helping because
I was only more and more confident that I was going to get caught.

I mean, imagine the kids getting together and listening to that tape!
"Come here, come here, Alfonso!"

Who knows what was on that tape? I couldn't actually remember.
Again, I'm a musician. I like to record myself sometimes. I don't know
if I was singing about students. I don't know what the fuck I was singing. Except for that one song about Maria and how she reminded me
of Kim.

"Come here, check this out, Maria!"

I remembered one morning driving to school after I had pressed
record, screaming at the top of my lungs about Patricia.

*"SHE'S A FUCKING CUNT! God, I need to stop eating at McDonald's.
I'm turning into a fat pig. Look at this belly."*

I sat up in bed. Imagined my songs posted on Facebook.

This could make national news.

I imagined Maria - listening and being repulsed – yet strangely fascinated. I mean, she *was at that age,* discovering her sexuality. This could be incredibly frightening. And ultimately, later in life, her hatred would take hold, and she would come back to sue me. Get me fired. Great.

I had to get a hold of the kid who took my Walkman.

10.3.06

The next day I went to school and saw my favorite student. He was standing over in the lunch line. I casually strolled over, jingling some change in my pocket. He was just standing there, looking at the chips.

"Hey ... Spencer," I whispered. "Hey!"

He turned around.

"Hey Spencer," I said. "Do you know who took my -."

"It was Eddie, Mister."

I felt a rush of dopamine. My dick got hard.

"Eddie?"

"Yes."

"Valdez?"

"Yes. He took it. He took it, Mister."

I stared at him.

I patted him on the head.

"Thank you," I said. I walked away. Then I returned. "Oh and Spencer," I said, "you will be handsomely rewarded for this."

"Yes sir."

I jingled the change in my pants again, and pulled out a quarter.

His face shriveled.

"For you," I said, putting it in his hand. "Why don't you ... go and get yourself a milk."

I walked away. *Eddie. That little fucker.*

I wasn't going to go to Captain America on this one. *Captain America can't do shit.*

So instead I found Mrs. Lansbury at the other side of the cafeteria. She was the other hall monitor, reserved for the senior teachers. While only four feet tall, she was tough as nails. Her heritage was Scottish, and she had this bright red, dyed hair, that stood out like flames painted on a Mustang.

"Mrs. Lansbury!" I said.

I saw her approach. Man, she had to be in her seventies.

"Top of the mornin' to yas, Heffelapfle. I see ya got your detective face on. What's buggin' ya?"

"That kid, Eddie," I said, pointing over by the lockers.

There he was. Over there. He looked so smug. Little bald kid. Looked like Charlie Brown. But he was obviously hiding something. And isn't it interesting how some kids seem so normal, but after you talk to them, you get the sense that there is something deeply wrong.

I remembered asking Eddie if he was going through my desk, back on the first day, when I first met him.

"No," he had said, with a smirk on his face.

"But I caught you," I said. "Why are you lying to me?"

He reminded me of Burke from "Aliens." Burke always smiled to your face, and his eyes watered, guilt-ridden, because inside that turbulent brain of his, he was ready to steal an alien back to earth.

"Eddie stole my Walkman," I said to Mrs. Lansbury. "And Spencer, that kid over there, witnessed the alleged crime."

She looked at Eddie, then over at Spencer, and then up at me.

"Good for you," Mrs. Lansbury said.

I nodded.

She leaned in, and started whispering, vigilantly. "Now watch closely. What we're going to do here, is get Eddie alone. Let's not take him out here in the cafeteria, in front of his friends."

"Why?" I asked. "We have him!"

"Because then he'll have his friends in front of him, watching him, egging him on. He'd be more likely to cause an 'incident'."

"Ohhh."

"So instead, we'll write him a pass from one of his classes. He won't know what hit him."

"Yes!" I whispered. "He won't know!"

"And then …"

"Yeah?"

"We'll take him to the office, privately, and put him in a window-less room."

"How long?"

"Oh, all afternoon. All day."

"Good."

"The quarantine will confuse and disorient him. Then we'll give him a newspaper from yesterday, that kind of thing. The phone will ring, but there will be nobody there. You'll turn the lights on and off from outside the door. What songs does he hate?"

"I don't know."

"Find out."

"Okay."

"Then we'll confront him. Tell him he'll never see his parents again and that he's going to jail. That is, unless he returns your Walkman."

I nodded, putting on my Darth Vader helmet.

"Yes, my Master."

10.5.06

Now I put on my imaginary Darth Vader helmet as a coping mechanism to deal with all of the kids coming at me, day after day.

See, my first quarter was *so* bad, what with the bomb going off in my class and such, that I was actually contemplating suicide. I would drive my car around for hours after work, saying *I can't believe this is my life. Don't tell me I'm locked in. No! No! No! Maybe it's karma for that girl I dumped back in high school. She would be laughing now.*

But all that quickly changed when I noticed that if I pretend I'm Vader, class seems to run much smoother. I would actually pretend to put on my mask when no one was watching. And I even breathed like him, softly under my breath.

I remember the day that Eddie caught me putting on my invisible Darth Vader mask. "Cuuu-dggge," I said to myself, making electronic noises. "Sssssssss."

I looked up from the dark corner. Eddie was watching me. But I was no longer me. I was Darth Vader.

"Eddie," I said, looking down at the eighth grader. "Hoooo-puuuuuuh."

He went running down the hallway.

WOW.

Fuck yeah.

This is awesome.

I read somewhere that Jeffrey Dahmer had similar coping mechanisms. After he was caught for eating 17 people, and drugging them and having sex with their bodies, he said that Darth Vader was his idol, because he was able to intimidate everyone around him. He simply wondered how he could have that power. And then he started eating people.

It's called command presence, Leo.

"I wonder if Jeffrey Dahmer put on a fake Darth Vader mask, too," I thought as I walked down the hallway. "You know, in the early stages. By taking this action, by pretending that I am Darth Vader, is this somehow taking the road down the dark path to evil? Am I somehow harnessing the dark side of the force, rather than the good?

"Maybe I should make a Yoda mask, too," I thought. "That would be a nice balance. Yin and Yang. Both sides of the galaxy that kind of thing. *But was Yoda ever really respected?* Not by Anakin. *Am I Anakin?*"

"Hooo-pppuuuh," I whispered, under my breath, striding down the hall with my invisible cape. "Where are the rebels who stole the secret to getting me fired?"

"I GOT IT MR. HEFFELAPPLE! I GOTS THE BAH-STARD!"

I turned around.

Lansbury.

She was holding the Walkman in her left hand.

I took off my invisible mask. "Cuudge. Sssss."

I opened up the Walkman. It was empty.

"Was there a tape in there?" she asked.

"Yes," I said.

"Kid says he threw it away. But I don't believe him."

At hearing this disturbing news, I reached out to choke her, but then held back.

Chapter 10

BREAKING DOWN

10.7.06

Who am I? Darth Vader? Sergeant Heffelapfle? What am I doing? How did I end up in Vegas? I can't stand my profession. I'm in a nightmare. I'm in a nightmare. I'm in a nightmare.

"Come down to the office, Mr. Heffelapfle," a voice boomed.

Get me out of here. FUCK! FUCK! FUCK!

"Sit down. Be quiet. Sit down! Be quiet!"

Oh my God. This is terrible. I seem to be stuck.

And where are all the girls Ed was talking about? Here I am, all alone in Vegas ... God ... I know no one. They said it's lonely here, but this is ridiculous. And last night, I almost gambled ... but no. I won't allow myself to touch those machines. If I touch them once, then I'll do it a million times because I am a compulsive freak.

So *bleak. So ALONE.*

This is terrible.

Goddammit! There are interesting people here who aren't SUPERFICIAL - I just have to find them!

But what in Christ's name was I thinking? Vegas? VEGAS. Fucking Las VEGAS? I remember taking a vow to my ex-girlfriend – that if I ever wound up in Vegas, she had a right to shoot me. And here I am, teaching at-risk, Title One, lower socioeconomic fuckups!

It's a perfect storm.

They want to fire me *already*. And I *want* to be fired. *This is terrible.* And everyday I come to work and face these little horrors. Again. I apparently can't get out. I'm *stuck … in some bad relationship.*

Oh my God. I've GOT to get it together. I've GOT to put more energy into this teaching thing and at LEAST stay here until my two year contract runs out!

TWO YEARS? JESUS!

No, it's no big deal.

You can do it.

MAN! COME ON! Seriously! God!

Shit. And *she* might come in. Patricia might come in so I have *got* to make this a smooth classroom. *I feel like crying. This is terrible.*

I MUST lose the FUCKING SMILE when I scold the kids. It creeps in too often.

I keep forgetting.

I was really onto something with that Darth Vader thing. But for some reason it really lost its appeal to me. Pretending like I was looking through a mask got old really fast.

10.8.06

So today I went back into Sergeant Mode.

"OKAY! I WANT QUI-ET! IF YOU'RE NOT QUIET IN FIVE SECONDS, YOU **WILL** GET DETENTION WITH ME TOMORROW NIGHT!"

The kids hooted in hysteria.

"Tomorrow *night?*" I heard one say, snickering, and then another. "Don't you mean after school, Mister?"

They loved to make allusions. "QUIET!" I repeated. "The first person who talks and I MEAN EVEN A WHISPER AFTER

FIVE SECONDS **WILL** GET DETENTION. FIVE-FOUR-THREE-TWO-ONE-!"

The class went silent for the first time ever. I put my hands together like a submarine periscope and even made BEEP-BEEPING noises. "We're at forty depths. A-3." This was how I looked for people who were talking.

"SQUEEZE," I growled. "DETENTION!"

"What?"

"I just sunk your battleship."

"But Mister! I wasn't even!"

"That will be fifteen minutes after school."

"But Mister I wasn't even…"

"Thirty minutes!"

She stared at me in utter frustration. "But…"

"Forty five."

"I don't even care."

"Linda, when I say quiet, I mean quiet. So please see me after class. We're going to call your mother."

"She doesn't care," she said, snidely. "Go ahead. Want her cell phone number?"

"Yes, but *after* class."

"I hate this class, it's *boring.*"

"Well, so are you," I said.

"I'm going to leave."

"Please do."

She just sat there.

Finally. Stupid bitch.

I continued my lesson. We were reading about Egyptian rocks. *How did they get them all the way from Cairo to build the Sphinx?* Reading this was my choice, because we finally got through a book called *"The River Maketh."* It's a book by an author who writes children's books just to make money.

You see, "children's books" are a huge market – so you get these publishers who apparently just slap glue onto paper, throw some random words down, and BOOM! They make a million dollars.

Normally I wouldn't force the class to read such vile trash – normally we'd be reading about poisonous spiders and snakes - but my mom actually bought an entire classroom set for me! And then she made me a shower of lesson plans! So what do you do?

I was at home and the phone rang.

"Did you get the books in the mail yet?"

"No, Mom."

I looked over at her boxes that were just sitting on the kitchen counter. Ostensibly, I was so tired after work that I had no motivation to do anything but read *People* magazine and eat chips. I tried to remember what life used to be like, before Las Vegas, before Darth Vader, but I couldn't. And it occurred to me that I would rather die than go back to work in the morning.

"Well," she said, "just so you know, I also sent you two books on depression. You really need to go and get some medication from a doctor."

"No Mom, I don't believe in meds."

"Well Leo, lots of stars are on them."

This statement is supposed to affect me how, exactly?

"Mom, I'm *not* depressed. Let's not go 'labeling' me. I'm just having suicidal thoughts, which means I've got to exercise more."

"Well you need help, Leo. I can hear it in your voice. This is not the old you. Do you want me to call up your principal?"

"No! I'm amazed you would even think of that. God no! Don't do that, Mom."

"What if I told you that I already called him and he's going to call me back?"

Long pause.

"Then I would tell you that you are trying in your own way to ask me if that's alright to call him and it's not ... It's not alright to call the principal!" I took a deep gasp of air. "Don't worry, Mom. I have a new plan to deal with the kids."

Chapter 11

DARTH VADER RETURNS

10.20.06

I decided to go back to Darth Vader. I felt really good in this new role. It really helped me get through the day. And yeah, sure, I would switch back and forth between Darth and The Tiger, a new character I created, who would growl and meow, but Dahmer was right. As Darth Vader, people really get freaked out by you, and you're the boss. This new me, I think, was sensed by Maria when she thought she could somehow run the universe unimpeded.

"AND WHAT DO YOU THINK YOU'RE DOING LITTLE GIRL? HO PUH."

She was in the middle of writing a note in yellow highlighter, but I was onto her little scheme.

"HO PUH. PUT DOWN THE NOTE OR FACE YOUR IMMINENT DESTRUCTION."

I pretended to pull a light saber out of my pants.

She ran out of the class, crying.

Oh great.

And into Mrs. Fiehr's room, too.

There would definitely be some type of meeting with all three of us right after class. *Good. Vader likes conflict.* I looked at the class through my imaginary computer screen, breaking up everything into grids, like how I imagined Vader saw the world.

"Beep-beep," I said. "H-9. Quadrant F-4."

However, halfway through the period, Maria came back into the room. Everyone started to cough and make weird noises.

"Coughing is not allowed," Vader said. "Ho-puh. Stop it."

I then captured a second note. It said some very terrible things. In yellow highlighter, no less. Maria had thrown it on the floor.

It said: **Stomp and cough if you think Mr. Heffelapfle is gay.**

I looked at Maria. *Rebel scum.*

She shook her head. "But I didn't do it!"

Lacey raised her hand. And in it was a yellow marker.

After class, Mrs. Fiehr came over to my room. The three of us sat in a circle. Maria put her head in Mrs. Fiehr's shoulder, and then pointed at me.

"He calls on me! All the time! He's *picking* on me!" she said, hysterically.

Mrs. Fiehr looked at me. I felt like I was in front of a judge.

"Now Maria," I said, smiling a little bit. "You're a little excited. *Here's* what happened. I looked over, and saw you writing notes. Then, you threw a sheet of paper with yellow marking onto the floor. That's called littering." I looked at Mrs. Fiehr. "Littering! Honestly, I simply could not believe you were capable ... of such ..."

"I didn't throw nothin'!" She stomped her feet.

"Right. But remember your Latin, little Maria. *Res ipsa loquitor*," I said. "The thing speaks for itself. I couldn't believe you would throw something, either - it simply made NO SENSE. Maria? Good Maria? So I didn't call on you to pick on you. Honestly, *I thought I somehow misperceived, ('Maybe Lacey threw the paper? Stewart? Rocket?')* ... I don't know, but then when I caught the note being passed around, that said 'Stomp your feet and cough if you think Mr. Heffelapfle is gay' that was written in the same yellow highlighter pen as the one I saw you writing with, earlier, I said, 'Maria!' because I made the inference that you wrote the note. I mean, how many kids write in yellow highlighter? None! Only you do."

Maria didn't say anything. She just looked at Mrs. Fiehr and shook her head, and then looked back at me.

"The yellow marker note on the floor is yours, and the yellow pen is yours," I said. "But it turns out that Lacey did it, anyway. So I'm sorry that I blamed you. However, you were still STOMPING and COUGHING."

"So were THEY!" she said, angrily.

"But YOU started this, the whole gay thing - you and Lacey."

"No!"

"Yes you did, you imitate me and act like I'm gay," I said.

"No! It's not just me! We ALL think that."

Okay.

They think I'm gay.

"You want to know why that is?" I said. "Listen, it's because I'm intellectual and in the Latino culture men have this macho ..."

Mrs. Fiehr jumped in, trying to stop me. "Now Maria, it doesn't matter what other people do. I'm telling you to stop. Okay?"

"Okay," Maria replied.

"... and people in this society are not used to males who are intellectuals," I continued anyway. "They all want the strong, silent type, and I'm sorry, I'm not going to change who I am because of this, shall we say, John Wayne mythos ..."

Mrs. Fiehr gestured towards Maria, hugged her, and wiped away her tears.

I looked at my watch, getting up.

"I guess the meeting is over?" I asked.

They didn't answer.

They were too busy hugging.

As I walked away, I could hear Mrs. Fiehr explain the idiosyncrasies of why I was perceived as a homosexual. "He's not gay ... some people just like to wear pink ... I don't know why he does, but that doesn't mean ..."

Chapter 12

ABORT ABORT .... RRR RRR.... GOING DOWN ...

10.29.06

There are some students I have not told you about yet, because there's too many to name. If I was a scientist, I'd have to name all the trees and shrubs to even get us in the zone of how many kids I had. Hundreds!

So I'm just trying to give you a synopsis here - one of these other kids was named Ivy. Again, if I was a scientist, and I found her in the forest, I would call her Poison Ivy. And that's because ... I mean, this chick would *not* stop talking after I asked her to STOP. Plus, I gave her numerous verbal warnings.

"BEEP! BEEP! BEEP!" I said, turning my hands into a submarine periscope. "BEEP! Ivy, what are you doing? Stop talking. That's your Final Verbal Warning! Did you not read the writing on the wall? Rule Number One says -"

"I'm going to sick my mother on you," she said. "Oh yes! She'll take away your job, Mister. I'm not playin'!"

"Oh yeah?" I said, daring her. "Let's give her a call."

"Go ahead, Mister. She calls you Mr. Buttfuck!"

I just stared at her. *Was she telling the truth?*

"It's okay to be gay," I said.

The class once again screamed in orchestral waves of sound.

I looked her mother's name up on the computer. And, while doing it, I made a mistake. *I confess - I did! My fault! Made a mistake! I admit it! I did what I always do when I see numbers.* I mumbled them.

"702-555-2368," I whispered to myself.

At hearing this, Lancelot started chanting, "555-2368!" (He looked around to see who was listening.) "Everybody write it down! Grab a pencil!"

Everybody scrambled for pencils and paper.

"STOP IT LANCE!" I shouted.

"702-555-2368! CALL 702-555-2368!" he continued.

"LANCE! GET OUT IN THE HALLWAY! I'M GOING TO PRESS THE BUTTON!"

I have two messes, no three, no four ...

"SHUT UP WHILE I CALL POISON IVY'S MOM!" I tried to shout over the noise, but no one was listening. Normally I tried to stop and deal with one problem at a time, but for some strange reason I just really wanted to nail Poison Ivy - once and for all.

That's strange, I thought. *Her mother's phone is busy!*

I looked up. Every kid in the room was on their cell phone. *Her mom is going to hate me.*

"How do you kids afford these cell phones?" I asked.

And then I heard the speaker.

"Mr. Heffelapfle ..."

Oh great.

"Please come down to the vice principal's room for your latest evaluation."

The kids looked up at me from behind their cell phones.

I went over to the button on the wall. "Yes ma'am."

The speaker continued, "We will send a hall monitor to watch your room while you're gone."

Make that five problems on my hands.

I found Patricia in her office. I sat down in front of her. She was typing on her computer. I sat staring at her for a good three minutes, until she rotated in her chair.

"A parent called in and told me that you have been handing out her phone number in class," she said, flexing her eyebrows. "Ivy Gomez's mother."

"That's ... not true ..."

Patricia placed my evaluation in front of me.

"Read it and sign, please," she said.

Now, I knew that it was going to be bad, but I didn't really care, because I don't *define* myself as a teacher. I'm a *musician*. There's nothing she can say in this evaluation that will bother me.

I looked at the leather bound folder and opened it up.

"Mr. Heffelapfle lacks all discipline," it said.

My eyes scanned down the page.

"His classroom is a mess. Gum and pop cans litter the floor. Kids run around jumping rope. And he seems to be completely oblivious."

Page after page I turned. ("They eat cotton candy", it said, "He's a little girl!" ... "He wears a pink shirt" ... "Why is he wearing a pink shirt?"). By the last page, I didn't care anymore. *But what exactly is "I"?*

According to Freud, only 10 percent of the human personality manifests itself as the ego, and the rest remains hidden. This hidden suppressed musician side of me seemed to suddenly refuse to stay suppressed.

Because... maybe she was right. She's the expert. Either you have it or you don't, right? I mean, there must be some Six Million Dollar Man out there who could take these kids and turn them into walking encyclopedias. Who was I kidding?

So I just said it.

"Listen, Patricia." I stared out the window, and then looked back at her. "I've been thinking. Is there any way to get out of this job without destroying my future career?"

She turned red.

"I'll look into it," she said.

"It's just too emotional for me, day after day ..."

I took a deep breath.

"And I think about getting out, all the time."

She nodded.

When I left her office, I went back to my shithole. *Only a pure maniac could work under these conditions.*

Chapter 13

THE GHOST

When I got back to class, I saw Mrs. Lansbury, my favorite hall monitor. She reminded me of a police officer. Just having her around made my classroom feel like a giant steel cage with inmates who could spring out of control at any minute. All that it took was putting the wrong guard in charge.

"They're animals!" she shouted in front of them. "No good beasts. Had to knock one of them in the head for ya."

"Thanks for watching my room. I'll take over the helm from here."

The second she left my room, *I mean the literal second*, it began.

New kid. Transfer student. Doesn't stay in any school too long. Computer lit up on this guy. Sixteen years old, flunked 8th grade three times. He seemed to be caught in a perpetual time warp. Name was Robert Cassidy, but in quotes on the computer it said, "Goes by 'Kid Cassidy'."

Kid Cassidy?

What kind of name is that?

In the first five minutes he was in my class, he began passing around an illicit note that said "Leave the classroom 10 minutes early" with a picture of me on it - a rather accurate rendition, I might add, except that I am not a retarded monkey.

"KID CASSIDY!" I shrieked. "That's not acceptable! I do no look like a ..."

"MISTER!" he said, while pointing his arms frantically. "There's a ghost in the room!"

"Don't change the subject," I said, holding his stupid note. "Focus."

"No! Look!" he said, pointing behind me.

I turned around. The TV turned on.

"Let me guess," I said. "The TV just turned on by itself."

"OH MY GOD!" yelled Spencer.

Ever since Spencer narc'ed on Eddie for stealing my walkman, it's true, he had become the teacher's pet. And he *was* always loyal to me. When other students made fun of me out on the playground, he barked at them (literally) and then waited for me by the purple pole.

But now he was acting like an idiot because of the new kid.

"Mister look at the TV!" Spencer said. "There's a ghost in the room!"

"No there's not, and let me tell you why ..." I began.

But before I could explain, a strange sulfuric odor filled my nostrils.

"Who lit off the bomb? What is that *smell*?" I asked.

I heard the sound of an aerosol can coming from the direction of the other bad boy, Billy Rodriguez. Billy was new, also. *The school was taking kids off the street, apparently, and putting them in my classroom.* He had recently come to my attention because he had tried to start a fight with one of the teachers.

"Kid Cassidy you're out of here!" I yelled, coming at Billy.

"What are you spraying?" I asked.

"Nothing," Billy said.

"Tell me!"

I heard Linda in the background. She was grabbing her throat and wheezing. "Mister!" she said. "I'm having an allergic reaction! Mister! Mister! Seriously ..."

"THERE'S A GHOST! THERE'S A GHOST IN THE ..." Spencer cried.

"Give me the perfume," I tell Billy.

"It's not me," he said.

"Listen, I'm going to click for the hall monitor, if you don't give it to me."

"Go ahead," he said.

I'm not going to fight with this kid, I thought. *There's something wrong with him, more than the other kids. I can see it in his eyes. He's dangerous.* I clicked the wall button again.

A loud beep came from the speaker.

"Yes?" asked a secretary.

"We have another situation in Mr. Heffelapfle's class," I said, into the microphone.

"What is it this time?" she asked.

"Some type of aerosol gas," I said. "Could be a WMD."

"Okay we're on it."

About half an hour later, Captain America finally came - and Billy still wasn't letting up. And now the room just smelled like shit. Captain America gave me a look like he was on top of it, so I could just relax for the rest of the period.

"Give me the spray!" Captain America yelled.

"I don't have it," Billy said.

"Where is it? Hand it over, kid!"

"I don't have it."

"Then shut your mouth."

There was a long moment of silence, as we all just stared at each other in my giant bouncing ball of a room. It felt like we were floating in space and words were suddenly worthless because someone had posed that there was a ghost in our presence. *Could it be possible that we weren't alone?* Spencer stared at the haunted television screen. Kid Cassidy watched us from afar, and took off his iPod.

Captain America wiped his face off with his handkerchief. The air conditioning was broken in my room, so I asked some kid to fill up a water bottle for me out in the hallway. I figured I would start spraying kids in the face to make sure no one passed out from the heat.

I looked at Captain America. His arms were folded and he just stared at my class, probably composing a speech in his mind to remind everyone of how fucked up they were.

But before he could speak, Billy raised his hand.

Captain America looked at me. I nodded. Captain America looked at Billy.

"Excuse me, Captain America," Billy said, unfolding his arms. "Can I ask you a question?"

"What?" he said.

Billy leaned in. "Do you have a high school degree?"

Captain America looked at me again. I didn't even know this information. He looked back at Billy. "Yeah, so?"

"And this is the best job you could get?" Billy asked. "A hall monitor at some middle school?"

The kids snickered viciously.

Captain America frowned.

I was about to jump in, but the kid I sent to fill up the water bottle came back, so I began to spray my face. It was *so* hot.

"So Captain America, don't you think you should have shot a little higher? So you just decided 'I'm not going to go to college, I'm going to be a hall monitor. I'm going to go back in time, instead of forward. I'm going to be a middle schooler all over again.'"

Captain America flexed the hinge on his jaw.

"You could be a doctor or a lawyer," Billy said. "But you're like, 'I think I'm going to be a hall monitor.'"

I looked at Captain America, who began to turn into pure liquid before my very eyes. The room suddenly began to smell like a men's athletic locker. Could it be that the kids could subconsciously sense the fear in him by the pheromones he was releasing?

"Is that you on your bicycle I see driving to work every morning?" Billy asked.

Captain America didn't respond.

"So you were just content with getting a bike?" Billy said, ruminating. "Most people are like, 'I'm going to get a car and go to college,' but you were like, 'I'm going to get a bike, go back to middle school, and become a hall monitor.' Was that your plan?"

And then Captain America just lost it.

"FUCK YOU! YOU LITTLE FUCKING DICK!" Captain America yelled. He held up both of his middle fingers, and backed out of the doorway, leaving me all alone.

"STOP IT RIGHT NOW!" I yelled. "Billy, that's INSUBORDINATION! LOOK THAT WORD UP!" I turned to Mariana, "Write it on the board so we'll all know what Billy is doing."

The metal speaker turned on again, "Mr. Heffelapfle, if you're on campus, please come down to the office."

Patricia. That bitch. She was calling me down like 10 times a day lately.

"Again?" I asked. "What for?"

The speaker replied, "We'll send Mr. Samson back down to watch your room for you."

"Okay," I said, pressing the button.

Minutes later, Mr. Samson, i.e., Captain America, walked back into my room. He looked at me, then at Billy.

"Was it alcohol?" Billy asked.

"Shut up," Captain America said.

"I'm sorry, Mr. Samson," I said. "But I'm wanted in the office. So I have to go."

He looked at me with a look that said, *don't leave*. He began to turn red again. We stared at each other as the door closed.

I heard Billy's voice as I left the room. "Where did the wrong turn occur, *Captain*? Seriously, I just want to know, so I know what mistakes to avoid in my life."

Chapter 14

ONE FAVOR

11.2.06

"We bend you to remain here in the comfort of our eye..."
-Claudius to Hamlet
(Act I, Scene II)

I walked into Patricia's office.

The principal was there. I had never actually met him before. His name was Dr. North. Used to be in the military, I hear. He was in his 50's, had a receding hair line. This strong cologne. Seemed like a nice guy. Looked like a nice guy. But we had never talked before. He had a pin of an American flag on his tie.

"Please, take a seat," he said. "I heard that you were thinking about quitting, Leo, and I just wanted to come down to tell you all of your options."

"Okay."

"Now," he said, looking at Patricia, then back at me, "this is not the first time that this has happened to me ..."

He stared off. "I used to fly Apache helicopters…"

I looked at Patricia, who closed her eyes.

He continued, "...in Desert Storm, and I lost a lot of boys there, too."

"I'm sorry, sir," I said.

"So I'm going to tell you what I would tell my own son."

"Which is?"

"If you quit before January 2nd, you won't lose your bonus sign on money."

"Thank-you, sir."

He shook my hand. "I'll probably quit," I said.

"Well you can hand in a letter of resignation now, or you can wait until Monday to sleep on it."

"I better wait," I said. "Talk to my parents, first."

"Okay, son," he said, patting my shoulder.

Later that night, I called home to tell my parents the good news and they freaked out. My mom was crying, saying how much it must have hurt being evaluated by Patricia.

"No, Mom," I said. "Don't define me. That's how *you* would react. Because you call yourself a teacher."

"I do."

"But I don't call myself a teacher. I'm a *musician.*"

She handed the phone off to my father.

"Listen," he said, in a rather harsh tone of voice, the one that says I'm an idiot, "what are you going to do then?"

"I'm going to drive to Portland and for the first time in my life follow my dream and become a musician."

"And what," he said, "hang out with a bunch of punks."

"Those are my peers, Dad."

"Punk rockers? Drinking beer? I'm sure that will get you far."

"But I have to, Dad."

He took a long breath of air. "Now listen. Society is very hard on artists. Now I could have been one too, but where would that have left the family?"

There was a long silence.

"So," he finally said, "I'm going to ask you for one favor. For all the things I have done for you in your life - raised you from a boy, taught you how to talk, and shown you how to play football ... For all the years I paid for your college that you threw down the drain - can you just do me one favor now, for your father, and don't quit your job?"

Long pause.

"I'll sleep on it," I said.

He handed the phone over to my brother. "Hi Leo I just want you to know we're all worried about you up here and we're talking about you over dinner and I want you to know that I love you and please don't quit and if you do at least wait until I buy Mom and Dad's car because I'll need it to drive down to work if you borrow money then they won't sell it to me I love you Leo."

"Okay, Gregor, thanks," I said. "Thanks for thinking of me. I love you, too."

He handed the phone back to my dad. "So you're going to stay there?"

"I'll sleep on it."

"Leo, if there's just one favor that I ask of you, it's that you stay at your job."

"Yeah, yeah, I know, I heard you the first time. Just one favor."

"Sometimes, sometimes, there is a time in a person's life that is uncommonly difficult, that tests your manhood. This is one of those times."

"Okay, thanks Dad. Is Mom there?"

He handed the phone over to Mom. "Did you listen to what your father said?"

"Yes. He doesn't want me to go to Portland because he thinks I'll become a punk rocker and do drugs."

"Yes. Well, you just went six years to school to get your Master's degree, and to give up so quickly doesn't seem right."

I took a deep gulp of air.

"Like your dad said, sometimes there is a time in a person's life that they don't want to go through. A time that proves trying. Your father's was Vietnam. This is your Vietnam."

For some reason it really bothered me, comparing my job to fighting a war like that, so I clarified, "No Mom, it's like fighting in Iraq. Vietnam was a long time ago."

"Oh. Okay Leo. Well, maybe you should write a list of all the ways that the war in Iraq is like teaching 8th graders."

For some reason, this advice really seemed to help. "Okay."

"Will you do it?"

"Okay," I said, wiping away a tear.

I grabbed a pencil and hung up the phone.

LIST OF ALL THE WAYS THAT THE WAR IN IRAQ IS LIKE TEACHING 8th GRADERS IN LAS VEGAS:

1. Much like the Iraqis, the 8th graders don't seem to want my help, either.

2. The US soldiers thought that they were going to be educating the Iraqi people, but wound up being policemen. I too, thought I would be educating, but wound up as a policeman.

3. "If there's one thing that I want you to do for me," George Bush, Senior secretly told his son, "it is to invade Iraq." "If there is one thing that I want you to do for me," my father secretly told me, "it is to teach 8th graders."

Chapter 15

MR. RYDER

11.12.06

The thought of suicide hasn't been such a present contemplation - it's just been sort of hanging there, suppressed by my ego. But now the thought has returned. You know the one. The thought where you just get in your car, and drive, man. You drive to Portland to start up that rock band and work in food service until you make it. You're not supposed to be a teacher. Your dad is talking rubbish.

This thought has slowly been gaining steam, ever since my encounter with a fellow teacher named Mr. Ryder. It happened only moments ago. I was at some teacher meeting, and at the end of it this fellow came up to me and said that so-and-so said we "needed" to talk.

Side note: I know Mr. Ryder. I have met him in meetings before. And I have avoided him. He is consistently condescending. He crosses barriers in conversations that need not be crossed. For example: When two males talk, alone or in a group, there are certain *understandings* that are unspoken, yet omnipresent.

I am, of course, referring to the world of hierarchies, or social dominance theory. A full-grown adult male has been aware of this world ever since he was a child, when his toys were physically stolen by the local neighbor-child. And then he became more aware of it when "she" was stolen, at a much later age, by a male who had a better car, or better looks, or more financial standing.

So a man is aware of certain standings and certain invisible medals that he is to be awarded at various stages of life. The invisible medal that I was awarded by the Legion of Men was that of Age. Yes, Age. An Age medal. And with Mr. Ryder, who is younger than me, I was always demoted.

In other words, this medal, or this understanding, is "I am older than you are, and thus I am wiser than you. Thus, I get to do the advice-giving, kid." If the younger male is giving the advice to the older male, he needs to do so with a sensitivity of tongue. The younger male asks permission to give advice. He phrases his thoughts like, "And I know you know this, ha ha."

I am *four years older* than Mr. Ryder. If we were in high school, I would be a senior and he would be a freshman. If I was four years old, he wouldn't even be born yet. He refuses to take into account that if there is to be advice-giving, then it is to come from me, not him. *Don't assume I want your child-advice, Mr. Ryder.* And if I do, then he needs to have a certain "sensitivity" to the Legion of Men.

This, he lacks.

So I avoid him.

Besides, he looks like a Monitor Lizard.

But stop. As I was just writing this sentence, the thought hit me to not continue.

I check behind me.

No one is there.

Not to get too superstitious, but Ryder said some shit that kind of scared me – and now, I'm just making sure that his dead-ass grandparents aren't hiding in my closet.

Let me explain because this probably sounds weird.

Okay.

So Ryder came to my room. And he talked to me about Patricia and how I needed to watch my back. This is all good because JC said we needed to talk. He had gone to the Union, and said I should get the Union phone numbers from him because Patricia went after him, too.

"But I only had six one's and you had nine one's," he said, referring to our evaluation sheets. "Which means you got Unsatisfactory, and I barely escaped with a Satisfactory."

"I have to take a piss," he said. "Walk with me."

We walked down the hallway to the restrooms, under the watchful eye of the surveillance cameras.

"Shhh," he said. "The Eye monitors everything we do."

I looked up and saw the electronic black eye watch us – motion-sensitive.

"Duck over here," he said, motioning to the men's room. "It's the only place we're safe."

"Do you know some guy named Mr. S?"

"The hall monitor? Yeah," I said, taking a piss in the other stall. "Everybody calls him Captain America."

"He's been visiting my room. Coming to help me out with discipline."

"He does that for me, too," I said. "How nice. A really nice guy."

Mr. Ryder rushed out of the stall and pushed me up against the bathroom wall.

"What the ..."

"No, no, no," he said waving his finger in front of my face. "Don't be a hero."

"I'm *not* ... *oomph*."

I tried to scream but he covered my mouth. "Shhh," he said. "You need to wake up, son. You've been living in an apocalyptic dream land."

He slowly uncovered my mouth.

I didn't say anything. But I stood there against the wall, stunned. After staring at me for what seemed like eternity, he let me go and ducked his head underneath the faucet of the sink. His face came up, drenched wet.

"What ...?" I began.

He wiped his face off with a towel. "Because Captain America is not who you think he is."

"What?"

He gave me a hard look. "He's a spy."

"What?"

"For Patricia."

"*No*," I said. "Mr. S and I are good friends - we ate Thanksgiving turkey together. I coach him on his relationships, and I've been trying to help him to stop drinking. We're even going to go to church together."

He slammed me up against the wall.

"Listen," he said. "Somebody's been playing with Loose Winnie."

"What?" I asked, shaking.

He let me go. "And how about that teacher friend of yours? What is her name?"

"Oh Anne Marie? My neighbor? She helps me with my lesson plans."

He grabbed me again, and put my head underneath the hand dryer. I couldn't see anything as the hot air blew in my face. Then he slammed me up against the wall again. I watched his finger dance in front of my face. He licked it and violently jabbed it in my ear.

"SHE'S A SPY! SPY! SPY!" he shouted.

"Fuck!" I said, holding my ear. "What are you doing?"

Oh yes, and add to my list of reasons why I don't like to hang out with Mr. Ryder: He slams me against walls, and dunks my head into toilets. This violates the rules of men.

"Oh sorry," he said, backing away from me. He tossed me a towel. "Maybe she's not a spy, but that's just the thing, see? We *don't* know."

"We don't," I said.

"It's just, Mr. Heffelapfle, you need to fight this. See ..." he said, staring off into space. "I have this inner voice ... that tells me what to do and what not to do. Cigarette?"

"No thanks," I said.

He lit one up. "I suggest you start listening to yours right now. Have you ever noticed it, an inner voice? In the calm, cold silence?"

"No."

"I learned to listen to it," he said, exhaling. "And that's how I survived. Got me through many rough situations. Worked in food service before. Should have been fired, but wasn't because I listened to my inner voice."

We went back to my room. The cameras followed our every move. *Whee! Whirrr! Kzzzz!*

Once inside the safe haven of my classroom, he sat back in my chair. Once again, he stared off. "My grandmother ... she was Cherokee."

I scratched my chin. Played with the tiny fibers of beard. Had I forgotten to shave this morning?

He pulled some sage out of his pocket, and lit it on fire.

"And she taught me when I was eight years old - to listen to my inner voice, and ever since then - I can tell something is going to happen, before it does." He wafted the powerful herb smoke on my body. "So if you can feel that Patricia is going to evaluate you fifth period, tomorrow at one o'clock, then she probably is."

He gave me a cold hard stare. "Then she probably is," he repeated, over and over again under his breath.

We watched the sage slowly die out. He took a long breath.

"Yeah, my students think I'm strange," he said. "They say I'm 'weird'. But my name in Cherokee is Hehoo Hasthe Chee Toes, which means, according to the chief, 'The Old Wise One.'" Again he looked off. "Or, Thunder Whip of Power. *Masada.*"

Maybe he is older than me, on a spiritual level, I thought. I decided to let him back into my Legion of Men with this newfound inner understanding. He was the elder and *I* was the child. *I was a baby in this new land.*

Wow!

I just changed my first printer cartridge. That took three hours! I had to switch gears out of writing these putrid lengthy lesson plans. They were due every week to Patricia. She wanted them to look like this:

"Lesson Plan: Power Standard 1.8.3, identify and correlate directions to complete a complex task inferring comprehension of similes and other modifiers [5.3, 5.5, NV 4.1, CCS 3.9]."

This is what the kids were supposed to do, I guess. Supposedly, by Nevada state law, we have to write all this shit on the board. Apparently the students are supposed to read these codes, and think to themselves, "Okay, this is what I am learning, NV PS 5.3 and 5.4. Complete a complex task inferring how to be a dick wad."

I reflected on my meeting with Mr. Ryder. *He was trying to tell me something*, I felt, and for some reason, for whatever reason, he could not.

"Well, as much as I hate Patricia," he said, "she sure has a nice pair of legs."

Wow. This shocked me. I thought Mr. Ryder was above women, because he appeared to be a sage of some sort.

"You know, I had not noticed," I said. "It's true that her sexuality had waned the moment I recognized that she was a robot sent from the administration to monitor my every move."

I then thought about it.

"If her and I fucked though, it would be great robot sex," I said, growling. "It would be like fucking a toaster. It would burn and hurt - as you put the toast in the oven. I would be so incredibly mad at her, slapping her for giving me those low marks and she would know that she deserved it. And I would love her for being such a hard-ass. I mean. Isn't this, in a way, what this is all really about? Her proving herself to her future employers about how tough she is, that she can handle getting a principal job, because she's really a man trapped in a female's body?"

"Yes young Anakin," he said, suddenly turning his voice into Yoda. "But beware the dark side. Anger, fear, aggression. The dark side of the Force, are they. If once you start down the dark path, forever will it consume you ... as it did Obi-Wan's apprentice."

Chapter 16
THE TEST

12.17.06

Eighth grade is a pivotal time for young English students because they're given all kinds of tests for No Child Left Behind. Failure to pass one of these tests means that they don't move on to high school.

They're very important.

I didn't know this, apparently.

Now it's possible that I had gotten so used to zoning out during our teacher meetings that are full of useless drib, (backpacks-good or bad?), that when real information came along I was simply *vacant*. That is one real possibility.

Another conjecture is that they simply didn't tell me. *And that life is a big joke meant to hurt me.* Here's what I remember hearing at the meeting we had in the library:

"Raaw raaaw TEST raaaw raaaw backpacks raaw."

And Patricia placed an orange booklet in my lap. "Here read this."

"Yeah sure."

I always got orange booklets. My room was piled up with them. Volume one, volume two.

"Did you read the orange test booklet?" Mr. Morales asked. He was this teacher I had little contact with, who had once been voted Teacher of the Year.

"No."

He laughed and waved his hand. "Nobody reads that anyway. No Child Left Behind."

"No Teacher Left Standing," I replied.

He laughed.

"I'll ... figure it out in the morning," I said.

"Smart man."

There was NO WAY that I was going to go home and spend my music playing time reading another manual filled with rules. The last time I did, again, I spent four hours reading about "Backpacks: Part four: A study by leading administrators." The chapters asked questions like: In or out? An analysis. Should they be filled? And if so, with what? If they're allowed in the classroom, what does this mean? A backpack full of ammo?

An Award Winning Study awarded by fellow administrators.

I had six years of this bull crap in college, while getting my Master's degree. You want me to read the orange book? Pay me overtime fuckface. I'm not a robot. Not yet.

"They're exploiting us," I told Anne Marie. "I'm a musician."

I turned on the paper shredder.

12.18.06

So I went to work the next morning, and found a note on my door to go and pick up the file box.

"What's the file box?" I asked some passing teachers in the hallway.

They shrugged their shoulders.

When I found Patricia, she was inside her office, staring at a perfectly piled pyramid of boxes, each individually color-coded with fingernail polish. She was counting them in a manner that told me many men had fought over the knowledge that they held.

"A-hem."

She didn't look up.

"This is your box, Mr. Heffelapfle. Did you read the orange instructional manual?"

"Yes I did."

"Did you read page 97?"

"Yes."

"Because most teachers forgot to read the highlighted square."

"Yes I did."

She froze for a moment.

Then she handed me a package of pencils. "There are exactly 36 six pencils here. Do not lose any of them. We need these pencils for future student testing."

"I won't."

When I got back to the classroom, I saw that there were six packets of 25 self-sealed packages. Some had student names printed in the left hand corner and others did not. Some names came on tiny post-it notes that I assumed were to be stamped at the time of testing.

Before I knew it the first bell had rung, and I still had not matched the social security numbers of the students with their secret question that had been given to them at the beginning of the year. Apparently they had been given secret questions. I don't know.

"Line up at the purple pole," I said, outside.

"What are we doing mister?" Catherine asked.

"We're taking a test of some caliber." I turned to the class. "TODAY WE'RE TAKING A TEST. CONTROL YOURSELVES."

HO-PUH, I thought. *The rebel troops are trying to deactivate the Imperial plans. I must crush them.* HO-PUH.

"Catherine, my pet, make sure that every student gets one of these pencils."

"Yes mister. And in exchange ..."

"Exchange?"

"Yes. Do I get to skip the test?"

"No."

Catherine seemed like a good kid. She really tried hard. But like all the other kids, she only wound up trying to hurt me in the end.

"Then clean up the motherfuckin' pencils yourself, Heffel-crapper."

I held my heart.

"*Catherine,*" I said. "I thought you were nice. But apparently not. Apparently you are not nice. You are mean. I feel sorry for your parents."

"Fuck you."

"Yeah well you can come after class for an investigatory meeting how does that sound?"

She didn't answer.

I looked at the class. They stared back at me, kind of excited to do something different.

"O-KAY," I said. "Let's take our seats and open up our test booklets to page one. Seems pretty self-explanatory. Begin."

The kids looked at me like I was crazy. "What about the math section?"

"Just whip through it."

"The whole thing, mister?"

I picked up a copy of the newspaper. "Yeah. Sure. You're in 8th grade now. This is important stuff."

This day was going to be *breezy.*

After about 30 minutes, some of the kids asked me if they should stop when they hit number 52. Well, the directions said to stop on 52, but we were going to continue tomorrow anyway to number 100, so it really didn't make any difference I felt.

"You can continue if you want," I said.

The speaker beeped.

"Mr. Heffelapfle, if you're on campus, please come down to the office."

This is a pretty tense job, I thought, going inside her office. All of her lights were dimmed, except for the computer, which filled the room with a strange red glow. This was different than the usual sterile lighting, I thought. She was just staring ahead, like something dreadful had gone wrong.

"Mr. Heffelapfle," Patricia said, under her breath. "Firstly, I didn't get any of the pencils back."

"Wait I can explain that," I began. "Kid Cassidy saw a ghost and then Captain America ..."

"No. I don't want any of your excuses."

She looked back at me with eyes that glimmered like she knew something that I didn't. Like she understood the true laws of nature, and I was somehow just another nice guy, which doesn't cut it in a universe that constantly measures whether you are weak or strong.

"Well what do you want?" I asked.

"Mr. Heffelapfle the students were supposed to stop taking the exam on number 52. ALL the teachers stopped their students on number 52. YOU let them continue."

I couldn't help but to scoff.

"DID THEY EVEN GET THAT FAR? Excuse me for saying this, but they would be lucky if they could make it past number ONE. My students barely understand English."

"MISTER HEFFELAPFLE! I have scheduled an investigatory meeting for you on the 23rd, which is in a few days." She turned away from me, rotating on her black chair toward the eerie glow of the computer. "That will be all Mr. Heffelapfle."

I stared at the back of her head.

"Thank you," I said.

But she wasn't finished. "Did you read the orange booklet?"

"Yes."

She looked at me, and then said, "Then why did you let them continue? On page 29, paragraph three, Section One, it says to make them stop. Let me tell you Mr. Heffelapfle, I have a child who is approaching 8th grade and I would NOT want him in your class."

"Well I would not want him in my class, either. How is he supposed to get anywhere if he's in my classroom?" I was suddenly struck with an epiphany. "I would not want him in this entire school!"

Her mouth dropped. She mumbled, "That will be all."

"Thank you."

Chapter 17

THIS TOO SHALL NOT PASS

12.19.06

We had another teachers' meeting in JC's room after school, but I couldn't stick it out, even though there were only two of us. She was so busy working on her crossword puzzle that she didn't notice my pain.

"Come on Leo, stay for the rest of the meeting," JC said. "We have important things to discuss, as teachers. That English closet is really messy. And, we gotta figure out a way to deal with No Child Left Behind because Patricia is going to act like those low test scores are our fault."

"No, I'm sorry. I can't stay," I said. "Today's been a really hard day."

"Well it's been a hard day for all of us -."

I tried to hide the tears but there was nothing I could do. This was starting to become a habit. *Déjà vu.*

12.21.06

This morning, I stopped by this history teacher's room, rather by accident, who taught on the other side of the building. It was that guy who I rarely see – the best teacher of the year - Mr. Morales.

After much conversation, and after I had spilled my guts about my dire situation, meaning Patricia and the investigatory meeting, I saw his face turn from bright to grim. Everything about him seemed tiresome. There were circles under his eyes.

"That's a shame," he said. "What are you going to do?"

I didn't answer.

His eyes seemed to be picking me apart to see where I was both emotionally and in terms of my thought processes. He ran his hand across his silver facial hairs, took a deep breath, and then poured me a cup of coffee. I could tell by a slight movement of his head that he was analyzing the situation from all sides.

"Just so you know," he said, "just remember, that this too shall pass."

"Oh I'm fine," I said. "I'm not too concerned with this afternoon's investigatory meeting. I'll have my union rep there. I'm not afraid of Patricia anymore. I'm used to it. I'm hardened."

There was a moment of silence.

"My dad always tells me that this too shall pass," I said.

"Do you ever get any positive feedback from Patricia?"

"No. She has not said one thing nice to me."

He shook his head. "Leo, I'm in such a ping pong situation between the administration and the teachers, you have no idea. But I'm on the side of you - the teachers."

Suddenly, I was so choked up. Mr. Morales seemed so concerned, so caring, like he could see right into me. How did he know that I had been feeling down? My mind raced on the fact that project Big Mouth - JC - had probably told him about my eyes welling up in the teacher's meeting.

"Thank you," I said, shaking his hand.

I walked back toward my room in a black daze, in no mood to even attempt to teach these kids because the situation just seemed too severe. Was there *nothing* one could do?

I was stopped in the hallway by Anne Marie, who was hanging out above the gym.

"Today's Friday, Leo," she said.

That's what we say to each other when we pass each other in the hallway.

"Yes," I said, laughing. "I had forgotten." I took a deep breath of air. "All I have to do is to get through today. I have an investigatory meeting on Friday."

"*What?*" she blurted. "Why? On what?"

"Because I didn't stop the test where I was supposed to. I said keep going rather than stop."

"*Oh my god.*"

"What?"

She stared off. "Well, they can *fire* you for administering a test wrong."

"They can?"

She leaned in, her eyes watering. Suddenly, for the first time, I believed that Mr. Ryder was wrong and that she wasn't a spy.

"Listen, Leo," she said, "when you go in there, you don't say a word - not a word, do you understand me? Don't volunteer anything unless your Union rep says that you can speak. Do not talk. Do not say a word."

"Okay."

She suddenly turned quiet. She clenched her fists and let out an acerbic whisper. Her husband came over. She looked at him. "They told him he is under investigation for not administering the test correctly. They can fire him for that."

She lowered her voice. "This puts me in a really awkward position. If they call me in as a witness, I don't know what I'm going to do." She shook her head. "I know what I'm going to do. I'm not going to go in. I'm going to say I'm not going in."

In between administering the rest of the tests to my kids, (I stopped them on number 34, as was assigned this time), Anne Marie told me to come and talk to her by the big purple pole.

"Is Patricia going to be the only one at the investigatory meeting?"

"Yes," I said.

"Well that's a good sign. I don't think that she has the power to fire you by herself. Only North can do that."

"Yeah, if she *is* the only one there."

"Where are you going to go, if they fire you? You'll only have one month's worth of rent."

I stared up into the sun. "I don't know. Get in my car and drive, I suppose, like Jack Kerouac."

She smiled, and then started to braid her hair.

"It's not the end of the world, Leo. The fact is, what you have going for you, is that a future employer can look at where you student taught - which is Anglo Saxon good homes Montana - and then they can say 'They put you *where?*' 'In Las Vegas, at a Title One, lower socio-economic gang school.' Leo, did you know that this is the *worst* school in all of Las Vegas?"

"Patricia forgot to tell me that when she hired me."

"Leo, it does not get any worse than this. This is the lowest rung on the ladder. These kids don't stand a chance. They should be reading 2nd and 3rd grade material, but you're supposed to teach them 8th grade material. Then they get bored because they can't keep up so they rebel."

I looked out at my car. I wondered if it could even make it back up to Montana.

"The odds were very much against you from the beginning," she said. "Somebody needs to tell what you went through - and they need to explain that you were the epitome of what happens to new teachers and the bad things that can happen to them."

After school, I stopped by Mr. Morales's classroom again. When he saw me, he clenched his jaw and his face turned red. He smiled, put down his book, and just started talking.

"I remember years ago," he said. "I had a substitute teacher. For 8th graders. Your grade. And I was so afraid to leave him alone with them, because I knew that they would eat him up. And sure enough, when he had to teach by himself, the administrators came over, saw him, and they fired him right off the bat. And so then, they just gave me his class to teach."

He stared off. "And no matter how hard I tried, I could not get his class to be better again."

"What?" I asked.

"Yes! See, what happens is …" he said, "is that the students see one kid get away with something, and if they see that he did it, then one more joins in. Now you have two rabble rousers. Then three and next thing you know, it is 10."

"Right," I said. "I was thinking about that yesterday, and how you have to stop it right away."

"Yes," he said. "Or they will become permanently out of control, and it happens very quickly."

I looked at the television. It showed a wave of water, building up steam. Soon there was a tsunami destroying Indonesia's coastline. People were screaming, and trying to get away from the water which was submerging them. Cars were being lifted and thrown into buildings.

He continued, "Benjamin Franklin once said that it is up to the teacher to teach, and not to teach behavior. But that is not the case, here. Here they expect you to be a disciplinarian, in charge of behavior modification."

I thought of those kids popping their mouths. How it all started out as one pop, and then another one would do it, and then another and another. Or they would do it with their coughs. Or they would do it with their pencils, beating on the desks, or stomping their feet. The same thing happened as they spoke, but instead of speaking, it would come in the form of just making little noises - yes, anything to add to the noise, anything to subtly destroy the sense of social order.

Chapter 18

THE ADMONITION

12.23.06

When I went into Patricia's office for the big investigatory meeting, I found her behind her desk, dressed in all black. She was sharpening her pencils and putting them in a little plastic cup. When she was done, she turned to face me.

"Did you bring a Union representative, Mr. Heffelapfle?"

"They never showed up."

"Okay. Good. Let's make this nice and simple. In my hands I am holding the Admonition. It is your job to simply sign the bottom. Not that you agree with what has been stated, but simply that you got it. Do you understand?"

"Yes I do."

"Okay then. Here it is. Please read each line more than once so that you understand the full thrust of what I am saying."

"Okay."

She handed me the Admonition. It was in a leather-bound black folder.

I opened it up.

THE ADMONITION

With the judgement of the angels and the sentence of the saints, we anathematize, execrate, curse and cast out Leo Heffelapfle, the whole of the sacred community assenting, in presence of the sacred books with the six-hundred-and-thirteen precepts written therein, pronouncing against him the malediction wherewith Elisha cursed the children, and all the maledictions written in the Book of the Law. Let him be accursed by day, and accursed by night; let him be accursed in his lying down, and accursed in his rising up; accursed in going out and accursed in coming in. May the Lord never more pardon or acknowledge him; may the wrath and displeasure of the Lord burn henceforth against this man, load him with all the curses written in the Book of the Law, and blot out his name from under the sky; may the Lord sever him from evil from all the tribes of Israel, weight him with all the maledictions of the firmament contained in the Book of Law; and may all ye who are obedient to the Lord your God be saved this day.

Hereby then are all admonished that none hold converse with him by word of mouth, none hold communication with him by writing; that no one do him any service, no one abide under the same roof with him, no one approach within four cubits length of him, and no one read any document dictated by him, or written by his hand.

SIGNATURE _____ DATE _____

I had never fainted before but my knees just buckled from underneath me. I woke up to Patricia's secretary pouring water on my face.

"He's coming to, okay, look at the light, how many fingers am I holding up?"

I heard a great wailing coming down from some long hallway, and a car horn in the distance, bleating. As I left Patricia's office, she turned out the light, and the secretary turned out the light, and all the lights went out until I was left in darkness, to feel my way out of the vice principal's office, crawling on the ground, in my own vile and shit.

PART II

Chapter 19

CHUBBY BUNNY

1.9.07

"You're lucky you can get these women, because you're young and skinny," Mr. Schendel said. "But then again, look at what these teachers turn into when they're older."

He pointed at Mrs. Pee. "She looks like a muskrat. Jesus. And look at her, over there. Mrs. Krushney."

I looked over at her. She was quite large. Long blonde hair went down to her waist.

"Oh God," he said. "When she was young, at least you could fuck her. But now, it's enough to make your dick shrivel up just looking at her."

The male teachers and I just sat there on the bleachers ogling at the other women teachers, who no doubt did the same to us. This was what happened before an assembly. One thousand kids sitting in an auditorium waiting to see somebody come in and talk about how to become a trapeze artist for the Circus de Soleil.

Schendel pointed to another teacher and started laughing to the point that tears ran down his fat cheeks.

"Looks aren't everything," I said. "You're a bad man, Schendel. A bad man."

"Now now," jumped in Mr.Hartman. He was the other young guy, like me. Just moved here from Utah. "My belief is that when I make love, I want to get to the point when my partner and I can wear blind-folds so that we don't have to see each other."

"Who would want to see that?" Schendel pointed to another teacher. "Do you have any of these blindfolds on you right now, because I would really like to protect my eyesight. At least some sunglasses…"

The secretaries, who unfortunately fit Schendel's description, stood up in front of the 900 seated 8th graders with their microphones, and began shouting into them, "OKAY KIDS, ARE YOU READY?"

"YES!"

"ARE YOU READY?"

"YES!"

"For what?" I whispered to Schendel.

"Um, I gotta get going," he said, and got up. "I … have … an appointment to go to. See you gentlemen later."

"What? Where are you going?"

I noticed some of the other teachers who had been teaching at Water's Gate for a while, getting up and leaving, also. JC, Mrs. Strictler, Mrs. Morris, Mr. Morales and Mr. Rollins - all leaving.

Hartman and I looked at each other.

"I'll need four teacher volunteers!" Bamby screamed into her microphone.

"Fuck that," I said to Hartman.

"Okay, Mr. Z, Mrs. R, Mrs. Pee, and how about Mr. Heffelapfle?"

I shook my head. Gave her a thumbs down sign and mouthed the words, "No thanks. I'm good."

That's when all the kids pointed at me. Kind of a strange feeling. And then they started chanting my name. *And they're not letting up.* No shit, we must have had this fiasco go on for five minutes.

"HEFFEL-APFLE! HEFFEL-APFLE!"

"Okay, okay," I said, getting up. Everyone squealed in transcendent drug-like bliss. "Orgy porgy," I said, jumping down the bleacher stairs.

I walked across the gym floor in front of the stadium full of kids. I clapped my hands. "So what are we doing? Good to see you, Bamby."

"ARE YOU READY TO PLAY CHUBBY BUNNY KIDS?" Bamby screamed, stomping her feet.

"YES!" the kids blared back.

"THEN BRING OUT THE MARSHMALLOWS!"

Mr. Z and I looked at each other, hesitantly. A sudden rush of panic curled through my spine. I noticed that the kids were getting extraordinarily excited about something, some to the point of spasms.

Mrs. Pee was about to say, "So what are we going to ..." but before she could finish her sentence, a marshmallow was crammed into her mouth.

"THERE'S *ONE!*" Bamby shouted. She put the microphone up to Mrs. Pee's face. "NOW SAY 'CHUBBY BUNNY'!"

"Chubby Bunny," Mrs. Pee muttered.

"NO SWALLOWING TEACHERS! IF WE'RE LUCKY, WE'LL GET TO SEE ONE OF THEM VOMIT BY THE TIME THIS IS ALL OVER, WON'T WE KIDS?"

"YEEEESSS!"

"In this trashcan!"

"YESSS!"

"Or on the floor!"

"YESSSS!"

"VOMIT VOMIT! VOMIT!"

Mr. Z was about to protest when a marshmallow was suddenly crammed down his throat. He tried to move back, but the mega two-ton secretaries came behind him and held his arms in place. Seeing that he wasn't going anywhere, I noticed he changed gears and decided to play along. He squealed, "Chubby bunny!" and pretended to sniff the microphone.

Unfortunately my acting skills weren't that good. Sweat was dripping from every hair, and I found myself wanting to cry. The marshmallow was placed on my tongue in the strange transubstantiation ritual, and I felt my scrotum sac shrivel as I voiced the words, "Chubby bun-ny," morosely.

Bamby furled her brow, like, "What's wrong with you? Get into it." But I couldn't, as I heard, "Two marshmallows. Chubby bunny."

"Two."

"Two!"

And before I knew it, it was "five" and then "nine" and "fourteen" and I couldn't say "chubby bunny" anymore because it was now "guh guh buh buh."

I used to always love marshmallows. In my childhood I would go on camping trips and melt them on top of graham crackers and Hershey's bars. I was suddenly really angry at the secretaries for making toasted marshmallows my enemy.

"Please stop," I tried to say, but no one could understand me. When the secretary gorged me again with one of her lubricious members, I said "Whose side are you on?" into the microphone, but everyone thought I was saying chubby bunny.

"Eat it," Bamby said, tearing the corners of my mouth as she rigorously tried to pleasure me. "Yeah, you like that, don't you chubby bunny."

Her limp legs showed underneath her nightgown, and when I recognized that Schendel was right, that this was my fate - droopy buttocks, fat dimples, and withered thighs - I suddenly couldn't breathe.

"Oh my God he's choking! Somebody call an ambulance!"

Chapter 20

THE NURSE'S PASSES

I woke up in the nurse's room. Apparently I had fainted.

"You'll be alright," she said. "Are you okay to go to class?"

"Yes," I said, sitting up on the cot. "Gotta … get … up …"

"No, no, lean back. Take it slow."

She got me some Gatorade and a small cup of nuts.

"Thank you," I said.

I had a cut on my forehead. She was tending to it with a Q-tip and a bottle of hydrogen peroxide. She took out a long white Band Aid and wrapped it on my head.

"Well, I dropped off some Nurse's Passes in your room, so if kids are sick they can use them. They're on your computer keyboard."

"How long was I out?"

"Only about 10 minutes, Mr. Heffelapfle. Just long enough for the kids and the secretaries to make you kiss their pig."

She held up a picture of me unconscious with an apple shoved in my mouth and a pig licking my nose. There was a trail of blood oozing out of my left eyeball.

"Oh good," I said, barely managing to get off the cot. "Don't touch me."

By the time I arrived to class, the students had just let themselves into my room instead of waiting out by the purple pole like I had conditioned them to do. AND. The Nurse's Passes. *The fucking Nurse's Passes.*

No…!

The NURSE'S PASSES were now MISSING from atop my computer keyboard. (Nurse's Passes to a kid, for your information, are like *gold*, because they allow them the freedom to safely roam the hallways. Technically, a kid would never have to go to class again. He or she could *live* in the hallway, drinking from the water fountain and finding bits of food from outside the cafeteria trash bins.)

I eyed the kids who just sat there, staring ahead, innocently. Of course, they had *no clue* what was going on. "My Nurses's Passes are gone!" I wanted to scream, but didn't. Hashim yawned. Angelo played with his eye. Ivy was quietly reading a book and Joshua was journaling, silently. This was all an act.

God, they didn't even seem real. They looked like zombies. A chill went through my spine as I remembered the ghost incident. *Focus.*

"Listen, you little … *goody two shoes*. You have one of two choices," I explained. "You can either return the Nurse's Passes, and not get in any trouble - I promise, you won't - OR we'll go through each and every one of your pockets until they are found. DO YOU UNDERSTAND ME?"

Silence.

I looked at my face with my pocket mirror. I was all cut up like Frankenstein. I put it down.

"DO YOU UNDERSTAND ME?" I shouted, even louder.

A sympathetic, yet hushed "yes" came back to me, as if from at the end of some long dark corridor. However, one kid was paying attention, and that was Harry, who was completely un-jostled, and riveted by the unfolding events. He had never paid attention to anything in his life. And yet my class was like watching some totally awesome reality show.

I folded my hands. "Now, just to make you feel secure that I won't get you in trouble, I'm going to turn around. While I am turned around, the person who stole the Nurse's Passes is going to place them onto this desk here," I motioned toward a corner of one of my large black tables. "DO YOU UNDERSTAND ME?"

Again, their "yes" came back to me, whiny and drowned.

I turned around. Stared at the kids in the reflection of the television set. "Okay, I am now turned around," I said.

The kids were staring at me staring at them in the reflection of the TV. "We know what you're doing, mister," one of them said. "We can see you."

"Huh? What? Oh, I'll look over here if you want," I said, ditching the plan to capture them. *It doesn't matter.* I instead stared at the chalkboard. "I'm going to count to five, and when I turn around the Nurse's Passes better be placed on my desk. Otherwise there will be serious consequences. One."

There you go, I told myself. *Whisper softly, carry a big stick.*

"Two."

They're finally listening to you. Command presence.

"Three. You better hurry back to your seat. Four. I'm turning around now but my eyes are closed you still have time to get away and ... FIVE."

I opened my eyelids.

"Thank you for the Nurse's Passes," I said, beginning to look down.

But on my desk, in place of the Nurse's Passes, was a tiny puddle that oddly resembled phlegm. The class stared back at me, once again, quite innocent.

I suddenly became infuriated. "Okay, who spit on my table? WHO spit on my table?"

I went over to the white button on the wall, and pushed it five times in a row.

BLEEP, went the sound from the speaker. "Yes?" said the secretary's voice.

"Kids … are spitting," I said, hardly able to form the words. "Help. Help me."

"I'll send someone down."

"Thank you."

I looked at the class just shaking my head. I still had that bad taste of marshmallow in my mouth. That was really a terrible performance I put on for the school, I'll admit. I just couldn't get into it. If I had done some warm-ups then I really could have jammed them down my throat.

The kids began to talk among themselves.

And for the first time, within seconds, there was knocking and Mrs. Lansbury opened the door.

"QUIET YOU FREAKS!" she shouted, upon entering.

"Thank God you're here," I said, pointing at the spit on my desk. "Look at this."

"Who did it, ya bah-stards?" she shouted.

"They stole my Nurse's Passes, too," I said.

She shook her head. "Your Nurse's Passes?"

"Yeah."

Her eyes scattered around the room, like she was hatching a plan.

"Do we need to separate them?" I asked. "Get them one on one? Dark room?"

"YOU!" she said, pointing at Harry. "Come here!"

"Me?" he asked. "Me?"

"No! Your mother! Get over here!" Mrs. Lansbury said, grabbing him by the ear. She dragged him out of the room as he flailed his arms, helplessly.

The class and I were left alone. I stared down at the spit. The class watched me stare at the spit. One of the girls, Cassandra, was apparently about to put a piece of gum in her mouth, but, so enthralled at the day's events, didn't, because the gum just hung there, outside her mouth, in her hand.

Seconds later, Mrs. Lansbury came back in and threw Harry tumbling onto the floor.

"IVY!" she shouted.

Hashim looked over at Angelo. "I told you Harry would narc."

Zounds! Poison Ivy! Of course! She had been in front of me the entire time! Well I guess that wraps it up for the Case of the Stolen Nurse's Passes. Some basket hounds barked in the distance. I looked over at Ivy who smiled an evil, hideous smile. I knew she was a bad seed. Telling me her mom called me Mr. Buttfucker. Of course she would spit everywhere.

"Me? Me?" she asked, innocently. "Me? Me?" I watched her slowly get out of the chair.

"You're going to pay for this one, and good!" Mrs. Lansbury yelled, grabbing her by the ear.

"Crime doesn't pay," I said. "Not usually."

Hall monitors can do anything they want, I suddenly realized. They can kick students in the face. So they get instant respect. And me, the teacher? If I say "crap" I'll get sued.

Once again, I stared down at the spit.

"Okay," I said. "Who's going to clean this up?"

"You are, mister," someone said.

Chapter 21

THE BIG MEANIE

1.20.07

"Even though you guys are spitting on my tables and throwing batteries at me," I said, "I have decided that I will not react anymore or let it affect me. And to show my dedication, I will prove myself to you by never yelling again." I raised my right hand. "I swear."

"Don't swear, mister," some kid said.

"Listen," I said. I waved my detention list around. "I've changed. For the better."

The class still kept on talking.

"LISTEN!" I yelled. "I'M NOT GOING TO YELL ANYMORE!"

The class shut up and looked at me.

"I always hated those teachers that yelled, and now look at me. Unfortunately, you give me no choice."

Once again, the class began to talk.

"SHUT UP!" I screeched. "SHUT UP!"

Once again, I got their attention.

This was very frustrating.

"Thus, I have adopted a new philosophy. A new ... how shall we say ... silver bullet, for my gun."

I waved some sheets of paper in the air. They had the words DETENTION SLIPS written on them in dark blue letters.

The kids rolled their eyes.

I continued, "Now, I know what you're thinking, another feeble attempt that won't work. Because when I say 'detention' you're going to say back to me, 'I'm not coming.' Right? Wrong. Because you have not readied yourself for me, when I say back to you, 'And if you don't come, then expect me to show up at your house.'"

"You won't show up to our house," one of them said.

"Yes I will."

"NO YOU WON'T," said another.

"Yes I will."

"NO YOU..."

"Yes! Yes! Yes! SHUT UP!"

But they did have a good point. "Listen, guys. I'll at least call. It will be calm in the middle of the night, when you'll hear that phone ringing."

The kids stared back.

"And your parents will get out of bed to answer it, and you know what they'll hear?"

"What?" Angela asked.

"Breathing," I said. "Because where will I be? I'll still be behind here, behind my desk, working at 3 o'clock in the morning."

"But WHY mister?"

"*Because I've got nothing better to do.* Okay? And I won't be able to sleep until I know that you're safely in detention, pushing a razor blade underneath my desks, cleaning off bubble gum."

"You've really got nothing better to do?" asked Roberta.

"Mister's lonely," Angela said. "We've got to find him a girlfriend."

But little did they know - I had a secret life.

1.23.07

Mr. Schendel had already set me up with a woman whom I had been dating for several weekends now. She was a counselor and was going to be a teacher one day.

We pretty much had a fucking relationship. And I didn't want this. It took me off my game. I enjoyed the fucking part, actually. But lately she was employing sex as a weapon, a control device, threatening to take away the one thing that got me through the day.

Oh, and she also went on a date with another man. Which may be okay, we are not committed, but for some reason it really bothered me. (In fact, I hung up on her when she told me over the phone.) And then she said she wouldn't step another foot into my bedroom.

And now, today, throughout our date some guy kept text messaging her. When I asked her what her plans were for the rest of the night, she said that she was going out to the clubs to meet up with a "friend." Then she laughed and said she was just joking.

So I had no choice but to tell Margarita goodbye. "Let's just end it now," I said. "Because let's face it. I would wind up breaking up with you later, anyway. Better now than later. And there's no need to be upset, because it has nothing to do with you."

"But I am upset," she said.

"Well, then that's your problem, and you'll have to deal with it. Just so you know I think you're both beautiful and intelligent."

She pushed my hand away, the same hand that only 15 minutes ago had limply tried to stroke her arm.

"It's just that the round peg doesn't fit into the square hole, that's all." I paused. "Besides, you won't come up to my room anyway, so what are you complaining about?"

"You just want me to come up to your room so you can get laid."

"Sure," I said. "And is that so wrong? We have sex all the time, and now, after you go out with some boy last night, you are saying 'no', and *joking* that you are going to go out to the clubs. But we both know that in every witticism hides a grain of the truth."

"But nothing happened with me and him!"

"I don't care," I said.

"Then why did you hang up on me last night, after I told you about him?"

"Because apparently my deeply suppressed Id *does* care. See," I said, motioning with my hand, "and this is the same reason that I want to break up - when sex enters the picture, you enter the realm of ghosts and demons. Things that were rational, are no longer. For instance, I don't believe that you're *not* going to go out to the clubs tonight, and I wonder what it's like, looking through your eyes, being a liar."

"But I'm *not* going out to the clubs tonight."

"Good idea to stick with your story," I said. "But do you realize that my GRE scores placed me in the top five percent of the country for thinking analytically?"

"What does that mean?"

"That means that your stories do not equate in my Harvard brain."

"But you went to the University of Montana, a third tier school."

"Yes," I said, "and it is because of that I am teaching at a lower socioeconomic ghetto school in Las Vegas sitting here talking to a broke Latino girl who only reads picture books."

Her face fell, shocked.

"It is quite ignominious," I said, and then added, "just joking," like a cruel bastard.

But it was true. I could sense it. She not only fucked Joe Hard-On last night, but that constant ringing on her cell phone was him, and she was now covertly planning to meet him at some seedy nightclub. *Obviously.*

Besides, I had bored her. We went to see "Capote" - a man she had never even heard of. While I was riveted, she fell asleep on my lap. Besides, she wouldn't let me fuck her in the movie theater. ("Why? Why? Why? Why?" "Stop it, Leo." "Why? Why? Why?") ("It's something which you have to do if you're the only two people here," I argued. "Can I pee on you?") But I made allowances.

"I don't know," she said. "You weren't like this when we first met. What has happened to you? It's because all you do is hang out with mean eighth graders all day, so now you're acting like them."

"No I'm not you stupid fucking trailer trash."

In truth, by ending it now I was looking out for both of us. I *would* break her heart, I thought. I *would* end it eventually. Probably as soon as I got my Yahoo personals account. And I felt bad, but not too bad. I mean, she didn't *read*. She kind of smelled. She wasn't the most attractive girl I've dated and she wouldn't even fuck me and she confessed she dated some guy last night and the pounding nightclub music in her car was a good indicator of where her spirit resides - and I will not have "energy exchanges" with someone whose energy I refuse to have. Complacent, lethargic, stupid, stripper-whore energy.

1.27.07

Sonofabitch. Middle of the night. Stressed out of my fucking mind. Can't sleep. Jesus Christ.

"I don't know, I've never experienced anything like this," I said, out of nowhere to no one, lying by myself in the middle of the night. I really hadn't. Nothing prepared me for this. I thought that teaching middle school would be a cake walk. I really did. Sure, and in some ways it *appeared* to be like that. But now I know.

The pressure. The *pressure* that we as *animals* exert on one another to perform. And that's why you see teachers, all fat and disgusting. Dressed in fucking rags.

1.28.07 MEANWHILE …

The assignment on my blackboard read:

"First Impressions: Write one paragraph about one of your First Impressions!"

I saw Alberto, one of the quiet guys in back, raise his hand from one of the back rows.

"Yes Alberto?"

"My first impression of you, mister," he said, "would be that you're a poor white guy. But now that I know you, I found out that you're just a mean teacher."

I took a big gulp of air.

"Good, write that down," I said. "That's the idea. Way to go, Alberto. THAT'S what a first impression is."

And then Maria got in on it. "My first impression of middle school was that I was going to learn in English class, but then I found out that I wouldn't learn nothing, mister."

"Maria!" I said, stunned. "Please raise your hand."

I looked at the girl who had made such an impact on my first year. The girl who at times haunted my dreams and made me think of Kim, the girl who had Mrs. Fiehr long for a daughter she would never have.

I looked at her, shaking my head. *Could she see?* Could she see my *pain?* I didn't care if Alberto said that I suck, but to hear this coming from her? My future wife? Wait, stop, again, she's not Kim. She's Maria. This is different. Regardless, now - that wasn't good.

So I just emptied my heart.

"Maria," I said, eyes watering. "Is it possible that you can be any more insensitive?"

She just stared at me, expressionless.

"Your words are … like daggers. And my heart is now cut."

I drew a picture on the chalkboard to illustrate. Blood oozed out of the ventricles onto the floor. I literally dragged the marker off the board and started oozing it down the sides of the wall.

God, she looked like Kim, suddenly. Right before Kim looked at me in the 3rd grade, right before I broke up with her. And the flood of tears came on, tearing me in half. *Prom king.*

Maria stared at me, trying to process my strange stare.

Finally, she said, "You have feelings?"

I didn't answer.

Ho-puh.

1.30.07

The secretaries called over the microphone to have somebody, anyone, take over period two for a teacher who was sick. I "owe" them a period because I was sick once. But I'm really fucking busy. Today is grade day. And I am a new teacher. Of course, secretaries don't really understand this logic. Their world is composed of making sure that the appointments are completed for Mr. Spineless, our principal, and that there are teachers like me available to cover other teachers who are sick and sell their "prep" periods.

Fuck them. I got my lesson plans ready. *They are bitches.* I'm sorry, but it is the truth. I like Bamby, but Carol is one neurotic mess. It takes nothing for her to get annoyed. And then, to top it off, she is extremely vengeful. (*Avoid vengeful persons* was the note taped to my mirror, growing up, back home in Montana.)

"Carol is mad at you," Anne Marie told me, out in the cold morning air while we waited for our students to arrive. "because you have not sold your prep."

"But there is no reason I should," I told her.

"Well it's an unwritten rule that when you are new, you should run down to the office and volunteer a few times. It's the *political* thing to do."

"Yes," Anne Marie's friend said, "it's the *right* thing to do. You just don't want the secretaries on your case."

"Well I kissed their pig and stuffed 32 marshmallows in my mouth. Is there not a limit to what they can ask of me?"

Anne Marie shook her head. "No. There's no limit."

"It's the *right* thing," her stooge assured me. "It's not about limits."

"If you're so into helping out the secretaries, why don't you do it yourself? That sounds like the right thing to do. The right thing to do is to take the pressure off the new teacher," I said. "Fuck off."

Wow, that sounded really good.

Oh wait, I didn't really say that.

I didn't even think it.

Instead, I just stared ahead, zombified.

"You're right," I said. "I'm going to sell my prep. There are no limits to what they can ask of me."

I felt my head, where the bandages were not so long ago.

Under the *avoid vengeful persons* sign it said *don't piss off your neighbors.* And I do like them so. Even if they are spies for Patricia, I don't care, they can spy on me all they want. Now that Margarita is gone, I'll like anyone who at least feigns niceness because I'm *starved* for affection. Who would like this person, I said, looking into the mirror.

No one.

"Okay," I said to no one, "it is time for some new rules." I decided to post them next to my desk in a frame so I wouldn't forget.

The Essential 18 for Teachers:

1. Pretend that these kids are picking on your little brother and you are here to protect him.

2. Always say to yourself, "These kids don't like me and I don't like them either."

3. If they give a smart ass answer, say "What did you say?" like you're going to kill them.

4. Remember that these kids try to not only hurt me, but my entire family as well. Why? Because if they cause you stress then *you* cause stress to your closest family members. And Mom can't handle this with her heart. If they give Mom a heart attack I WILL SINGLE-HANDEDLY KILL THEM ONE AT A TIME WITH A GIANT SWORD.

7. These "kids" have ruined countless days of yours. Remember that these are the same "kids" who bring you excruciating

post-traumatic stress syndrome when you get off of work. Maria is a fucking bitch and she must be destroyed.

8. These kids and their horrible behavior destroy lives and end otherwise peaceful marriages. These are NOT kids, they are NOT nice, they are jerks.

9. These are demons that have possessed the bodies of kids who were once kids.

10. Never be nice.

11. These are vermin, these are evil monsters, they are not even real people - whose mission is to spread their creative maladjustment syndrome. So attack the alpha - Lancelot or Portia or Ramona. Use whatever object you have nearby. Say, "You better knock that grin off your face. I am not someone you want to mess with. If you keep it up we'll call up your mom and I don't think she'll be too happy when I ask her to sit next to you in class. How will that feel having your mom sitting next to you in the 8th grade? I have a lot of parents doing it right now, don't think you're immune. NONE of you are immune."

14. Play it like a chess game. Yes, study chess. Get inside the warlord's mind. Study Napoleon and Alexander the Great. King's pawn white to G4 is handing out a worksheet before they even get into the class. Yes this is a game of distractions. Then nail them with another worksheet and another worksheet. Make the rats drown in vocabulary that they'll never understand.

16. Imitate Mrs. Fiehr. Notice how she says "I". It's "*I* didn't excuse you yet." She also says "NOW" a lot. "Spit out your gum NOW." Constantly ask yourself, when she is around, "WHY is she so scary?" Mimic her actions. She scratches her nose, you scratch your nose. Buy a long scraggly gray wig. Find a subservient husband.

18. Scare them by eating chalk. Get some of the pink chalk from your desk, take a bite out of a slab, and say "Mmm. Strawberry."

1.31.07

YOU ARE NOT MY BUDDY, a sign hung up on the wall.

"You're not my buddy, my friend, or my peer," I said, pointing to the giant sign. "WHAT does a BUDDY do? Manuel?"

"Huh? What?"

I ignored him. "Lancelot, what do you do with your buddy?"

"You get high with him, mister."

"That's right," I said. "And I am not going to get high with you! Why is that do you think? IT'S BECAUSE I HATE YOU."

I thought of the priest from "The Exorcist". Every time he visited the devil, in the form of that little girl, his hair would turn grey.

I looked at my hair. Yeah there's one. I plucked it out. This was another one of those long drives home, totally disgusted. "IT'S BECAUSE I TOTALLY HATE YOU. I HAAAATE YOOOUUU!"

Jazz music pumped out of my stereo. There was a time I really liked jazz. It kind of reminded me of hot summer days. Ah yes, Alexandria. I remember going to visit her, high on Tylenol Cold Medicine, just laughing and singing and whistling on my bike, up in Montana. Birds everywhere. Playing guitar.

Those were the good old days.

I continued to drive.

Suddenly, in the corner of my eye, I caught a glimpse of a sign that said "SUPER MASSAGE: Chinese and Tsunami." I slowed the car down. I've been seeing these signs everywhere. They're on every street corner.

What the hell is a tsunami?

I looked down at my balls.

No. I can't afford that.

I really needed a release.

It would be a travesty to give some kid from Montana $50,000 for his first job, and then put jerk off chains on every single street corner. *How is he supposed to save that money?* Especially if he's teaching kids?

I mean, you get off of work and you're like in the Twilight Zone. *A fucking toxoplasmosis trance.* A whole other universe. And there are no women anywhere.

"IT'S BECAUSE I TOTALLY HATE YOU" is going through your mind.

It's like you become suddenly *possessed.*

"CHINESE MASSAGE MAKE YOU FEEL BETTER MISTER."

And there's this hot Chinese woman, all oiled down on the poster. You can't tell how old she is, but it doesn't matter, because she has four arms and four bottles of lube oozing out of the bottles and onto the floor. Her third eye tells you she means business and she has a mouth that could blow an exhaust pipe off a semi.

"Well we could do that and then go buy a DVD and get some Chinese food," you say to yourself. "Take myself out on a date."

Chapter 22

KID CASSIDY AND BILLY VS. ME AND CAPTAIN AMERICA

2.5.07

TODAY'S ASSIGNMENT:

Would you defend someone who is getting picked on? Write one paragraph. (One paragraph equals at least 5-7 sentences in this case!)

Yesterday I pounded a stake into Kid Cassidy's heart. Not that I wanted to. But he wouldn't stop when I said, "STOP."

Kid Cassidy looked like Michael Jackson and he even had on one of those Michael Jackson gloves. He would make squealing sounds if you got too close to him, kind of like a guinea pig being squeezed to death by a boa constrictor. When you asked him to stop, he would tell you to "Beat it. Just beat it."

I had met with his mother on several occasions. She was really nice, and really young, and I could see that he was making her life a total hell. He was terrorizing his older sister as well, and he was about to be thrown out of his home. It was just a nightmare. But amidst all this, here's this kid who shows real potential. He loves his drum machine, and has a knack for telling stories. He should be getting challenged, but he's been placed in this shit can school that can't meet his needs. Plus he's got massive ADHD or something like that ... he reminded me of a mini artist. Destroy or create. But in this case, it was simply destroy.

I could empathize with him. So I let him do some things that other kids couldn't do, like listen to his iPod. But he couldn't even keep that under control. It was just sad.

"Kid Cassidy. Kid Cassidy," I said, but he wasn't listening to me. He couldn't *hear* me over the sound of his iPod. "Excuse me, sir ..." I said, making hand motions in front of his face.

"Me?" he said.

I nodded up and down.

He took off his headphones.

"Kid Cassidy, I'm going to have to ask you to take those off ... because ... well, the headphones appeared to sedate you, but now I see that it is only temporary, and you are abusing the privilege, with that squealing thing."

"Okay then. Okay then," he said. I saw an aggressive look take shape in his eyes. "Let's see what happens. See what happens to you and your *classroom*."

"Okay then," I said. "Let's see what happens to you when you get sent down to the Dean's."

15 minutes later ...

"I don't care. Send me. SEND ME!"

"Quiet," I say. I turn away from him, and begin expanding on subject-verb agreement.

"Personally..." I begin.

Kid Cassidy barks.

I ignore him. "Personally, I just write down whatever word sounds right: is or are, wherein 'are' is a singular verb. We all know this, heh

heh. This method may sound contradictory at times, and it seems to be, but just hold on, as I detail ...”

“Spencer is a NERD,” Kid Cassidy shouts in that trademarked high squeal of his. “Dancing to Spencer is like subject-verb placement to you, Mr. Heffelapfle. Neither of you get it.”

“Kid Cassidy!” I shout.

“I’m not a nerd!” Spencer shouts from under his glasses.

“I’m not a nerd,” Kid Cassidy says, imitating him. *“Help me put some tape on my glasses.”*

“I understand subject-verb agreement,” I say.

“Leave me alone!” Spencer shouts.

“Yes,” I agree. “Leave us alone.”

“Hey Mr. Heffelapfle,” Kid Cassidy says, “does Spencer remind you of yourself when you were his age?”

I look at Spencer in the corner with his Bible and construction paper. He’s cutting out a thorn hat with a plastic pair of blue scissors. His desk is cluttered with books on how to draw Moses and his disciples from the perspective that Moses and his disciples are ducks. And it appears that the girls are keeping a marginal 20 foot distance away.

“Sure,” I say. “Why not. Yes, Spencer was a lot like me.”

“Were you picked on a lot then, mister?” Angela asks. Oh great. The rest of the class is getting into it.

“Sure,” I say, “back in the 7th grade.”

“How come, mister?”

“Getting picked on is a character builder,” I begin to lecture. “Apparently Alexander the Great got picked on before he took over Europe. Everybody goes through it once, kind of like that song, ‘Everybody plays the fool.’”

“And you were the fool, mister?” she says.

“No. Anyway. Everybody focus,” I say. “We need to finish our worksheet.”

“Hey Spencer,” Kid Cassidy jumps in, “take a good look at Mr. Heffelapfle because that’s who you’re going to wind up as.”

"Shut up you fucking bitch! Leave me alone you nigger ass!" Spencer shouts.

The class does their "oooo." I turn to Kid Cassidy, and say, "Ssssh ... put your headphones back on, you win, ssshhh" but before I can press the play button on the iPod for him he screams at Spencer.

"I'll kick your little nigger nerd ass so bad you'll never want to leave the bathroom where you jerk your little pecker off to pages of the Bible."

"Kid Cassidy!" I command. "Get in the back corner!"

"I'm not going ANYWHERE if *Spencer's* not!" he says.

"No," I say. "Go back there or I'll call the Dean's."

All the kids are in hysteria mode now, shouting, "That's not fair! Punish Spencer too!"

"I'm not going to *answer* that. I'm not going to *argue* with you."

"Do you know why Mr. Heffelapfle sticks up for Spencer?" Kid Cassidy says. "Because after class Mr. Heffelapfle's going to take out his lube and fuck Spencer up the ass! They do it to each other! They're *butties*."

"Kid Cassidy," I say, as horrified as I can muster, "you just sealed your doom."

I hit the call button on the intercom. As usual, no answer.

"They're sick of you," Angela says.

BEEP. Finally. "Hello? Main office," rings the voice.

"Hello, this is Mr. Heffelapfle. Could you please send down a hall monitor, like Mrs. Lansbury, for Kid Cassidy Nelson?"

BEEP. "Will do."

I turn back to Kid Cassidy, who has his desk turned over and appears to be making love to it. "Oh Spencer, oh Mr. Heffelapfle, slap my ass-"

"FUCK YOU PIECE OF SHIT!" Spencer erupts.

"Stop it," I say, insisting. "Put your headphones on."

And then the door.

Knock-knock.

"Sh. Quiet." I whisper harshly at the entire class.

Surprisingly, they all get quiet.

We all look at the door.

I hate these moments.

Who could it be? It *could* be Mrs. Lansbury. Hell, it could be the Superintendent.

"*Don't you say a sound,*" I say under clenched lips to the class.

I tuck in my shirt. Comb my hair in the mirror.

"Come in," I say.

The door swings open. Captain America. And he's high.

"CAPTAIN AMERICA!" everybody yells.

"What's the situation here?" he asks, hands out and waving.

"Kid Cassidy," I say, motioning. "Told me to lube up and give it to that kid, Spencer, over there. And Spencer's not even like that."

Captain America nods, taking in what I am saying. He rubs the cross around his neck. There is a nice new coat of wintery dandruff building up on his shoulders.

"Come here," Captain America says. He takes me by my arm. We walk over to a side desk, about 10 feet away from the kids, and he starts whispering in my ear. His breath is pretty intense, like Vodka, coffee, and weed. The class has become quieter than I have ever heard them.

"Listen," Captain America says, covering his mouth. "Here's the situation. Kid Cassidy is in our office, in the Dean's *constantly*. So what I'm going to have you do is fill out a counselor form."

He hands me a blue form.

"But isn't this a step *backwards?*" I whisper. I look over at Kid Cassidy who has begun to squeal again. "I've sent him to the counselor a million times. Next in order is the Dean's."

"Yes, but we've got to play the Game."

"He told me to shove that kid's prick up my asshole."

"I know I know. But we've got to work with him."

"I let him listen to his iPod in class. I don't let anybody else do that. I let him bring food to class, and I turn my head. I've seen him touch other girls' breasts. Yeah, I'm not joking. I let him cross kick Spencer in the face. And we both know that he's the one who's been taking pisses in my corner! *And I didn't say anything!*"

"I know I know," he says.

"I'm kidding," I say. "Partially ... but you get the point. I don't let him kick Spencer. I was just joking about that part."

"Just keep him in your class," he says, and then says, louder, "Okay guys - you only have 15 minutes left, 15 minutes left, so show Mr. Heffelapfle some respect and let him *teach* you. That's what he's here to do, to *teach* you ..."

And then he leaves.

"Thanks for your help, Captain America," I say.

Kid Cassidy starts spanking the desk again. "Ooooh YESS!"

I turn to Spencer. "Listen, Spencer, I'm sorry, but you see what we're up against. I've filled out all the forms."

"I'm scared," Spencer says, looking at Kid Cassidy. "He's going to kick my ass as soon as I get out that door."

"I don't know what to tell you. Take up martial arts, or something. This is how the great ones started."

2.6.07

Every morning Captain America and I eat donuts in the teacher's lounge. "Stop trying to do what I do," he said.

Funny thing is, I'm genuinely scared of turning into him. No car, no girlfriend, a fat hall monitor who thinks that I can't tell that he's high out of his mind. Sits at home on Saturday night, playing guitar all alone. All the teachers talk about him behind his back. ("I see that they're hiring ex-prisoners on parole," JC said, pointing at him out on the playground.)

Why do hall monitors get such a bad rap? Maybe they should change their title. How about "conflict-resolution social worker." Hall monitor sounds too much like all you do is break up fights. On the other hand, that's what he does. And the world is riding on the line.

"I got in the middle of it," Captain America told me. "I got into a *fight.*"

"Oh, that's nice."

Apparently he *was* in the middle of the fight, I heard from other teachers. "I saw it," Mr. Morales told me, in passing. "Mr. S was out there exchanging blows with 8th graders. Said something about how he's not going to wind up as a hall monitor."

I never saw Mr. Morales much. Maybe just quickly, out in the parking lot after school. He had to yell over the wind. "This is how it all starts," he said.

It's never this windy here in Vegas. Spring is on its way.

"There's going to be a fight and then there'll be paybacks," he continued, rubbing his arms from the cold. "This year it's going to be Blacks versus Latinos. And soon there will be weapons."

"At least it's not Blacks and Latinos versus teachers."

"Oh," he said. "There will be that too."

2.10.07

Meanwhile the jerk-off chain store was becoming real old. Dr. Phil was telling me I'm better than all this, day after day. I really needed Margarita, but she was ignoring my phone calls. I imagined inventing a device made out of a feather attached to a string attached to some coat hangers. When the fan was turned on, it would gently tickle your back. Then all I needed to have was the voice of Alexandria whispering in my ear that she really loved me and I would become a great musician one day.

HA!

What a dream. I need to *pick it up*!

I decided that I would get up at midnight from now on. Yes, get up at midnight, work on my music all night, go teach school all day, come home, take a dip in the pool, and go to bed at 4 p.m. Then repeat the process.

That would be six hours of straight work on my music.

And in exchange for working so hard? Well, I could go visit the freaks in the desert or see what Vegas nightlife was really all about. Hell, maybe the gods would hear my cries, and they would come to me.

Chapter 23

BILLY'S PARENT TEACHER CONFERENCE AND ANOTHER INVESTIGATORY MEETING

2.13.07

And so then came the day I got into the entanglement with Billy. I mean, I couldn't handle him spraying that horrid cologne in the room anymore. We don't have windows.

But that's not the reason we had our entanglement. Apparently he was going to hit Spencer. But this wouldn't happen on my watch. I owed Spencer a favor for finding my walkman.

I looked up from my desk. Billy. He was on the prowl again, and had found a target for his derelict tendencies. He had his fist raised toward Spencer's face. Spencer was on the verge of tears. I had to do something. This was one of those big moments. Now was my chance to save the day. And so I did.

"Don't," I said, with all the fervor I could muster. My eyes were rolling in back of my head.

"Oh I will if he doesn't give me my pencil back," Billy said.

"I DON'T HAVE YOUR FUCKIN PENCIL!" screamed Spencer.

Kid Cassidy looked at me. "See? You should have let me listen to my iPod."

"But that was weeks ago, Kid Cassidy," I said.

"I don't care," he said. "You didn't listen. Now look at your 'classroom'."

"Oh god, this again? You never give up! It's always something with you, isn't it?"

"I'm going to hit him," Billy said, raising his fist toward Spencer's face.

"You better not hit him," I said. "Or I'll hit you."

I could tell that my words really affected him, because he immediately hit Spencer in the arm and then threatened to hit him in the face.

Billy then turned toward me. "What did you say? What did you say Mr. Buttfucker?"

"That's Heffelapfle."

He strutted up to my desk, put both hands in the air, and began dancing around like Muhammad Ali. "Come on. Let's go. Let's go right now, pussy. Come on."

I rolled my eyes. "I admire your enthusiasm. Sit down."

"Come on. Come on fucker."

"Sit down. Let's put that energy into our root words."

"Come on, fucker."

"The root word of 'fuck' means 'to make'."

"I'm going to sue you for saying you were going to hit me."

"Sit down."

After class I set up a parent teacher conference to see if we should have the boy euthanized.

2.15.07

"Mr. Heffelapfle, if you're on campus, please come down to the office."

My favorite words, I thought, taking a shit. They played on the speakers like a rock song.

As I was walking out of the restroom, I practically hit Patricia with the door. What was she doing right outside the men's room? No matter, because she told me that she had to leave all morning and thus would miss the parent teacher conference, thank God. Apparently she had to terrorize Mr. Ryder for something.

I went into the meeting all by myself only to find Billy there with his mother. She was a tiny woman. Her son towered over her. Mr. Hartman was called in to translate.

Billy's mother began talking. She raised her fist in the air and jabbed it wildly.

Hartman translated her words to me, "She says that Billy tells her that you were going to punch her son."

Hartman looked at me like he couldn't believe her words.

"Whoa, wait," I said. "Let's back up here."

I straightened out my collar. Took a deep breath. Turned toward Mrs. Rodriguez. "Your son, Billy, had picked a fight with a fellow student. He punched this fellow student in front of me, while I was actually watching him. Hard. And then while looking at me, he tells me he's going to kick my ass."

Hartman nodded, and translated this to Mrs. Rodriguez.

I continued, "And so *I* say, 'If you punch him, I'm going to punch *you*.' That's all."

He translated this. Then he said, "She says that that is not right, you should not have done that."

I turned to her, and said, "That's right. That was an accident, and I am sorry. I should have said I would have kicked him." I looked at Hartman and he nodded, approvingly. "But the bottom line is, is that we are addressing a larger issue here, and that is the fact that Billy is constantly picking fights inside my classroom. And I want him to move up to the front row."

Hartman translated this. Mrs. Rodriguez talked to her son, who was shaking his head. "The mother says that he refuses to move up to the front row."

"Well it doesn't matter if he doesn't want to. I am the teacher, and I create the seating chart," I said to the mother.

Hartman translated this. Again Billy shook his head. "He's not going anywhere," Hartman said.

"Well why don't you come in and supervise Billy?" I told the mother. "Because I'm not a babysitter and he's causing trouble sitting in the back row. I often have parents come in and sit next to their kids for my classes."

(This has never happened).

"And we'd be happy to have you. What are you doing every morning at 9:15?" I asked.

Billy didn't like the look of this. Mrs. Rodriguez reached into her purse and grabbed her cell phone.

"She's calling the father," Hartman said.

Mrs. Rodriguez gave the phone to her son. I could hear the father yelling at him. Billy began to cry. He put his head under the desk, so we couldn't see his tears.

"No," Billy told his father. "I'm not moving."

Billy hung up the phone on his father. He looked at us. "The line went dead."

I could see that a counselor, Mrs. Lovely, had walked in. She interrupted, "Billy. We'll give you three seats from the front. How does that sound?"

There was a long silence.

"Okay," Billy said, faintly smiling.

At the end of the day, as I sat typing into my computer, I got a message from the intercom. "Mr. Heffelapfle if you are on campus, please come down to the office."

Patricia.

I went down to her room. "You may come in," she said.

"Yes?"

She handed me a form. "We're going to have another investigation next week to discuss allegations that you said that you were going to hit a fellow student. You may bring a Union representative."

"Thank you."

2.20.07

The week went by rather quickly. I was pretty sleep deprived because I had been getting up every day at midnight and working on my music. I would take a quick half hour nap before work and then drive to school, ready to do battle with Patricia.

I called the Union and they sent a representative named Carrie, who met me outside Patricia's office for the big meeting. She seemed quite relaxed. She had a double latte in her hand.

"Just answer yes or no," Carrie told me.

"Right," I said.

She was pretty hot.

"Don't argue. Don't say any long opinions. Don't get emotional. It's only one meeting of your life."

"Right," I said. "Thanks."

We went inside the vice principal's office and closed the door behind us.

Patricia smiled at the Union Rep. "So nice to meet you," she said. "Nice to meet you."

"Okay, let's get down to business," Patricia said. "Just give me a second to grab my notes."

We watched as her notes came off the computer. Page after page after page. The suspense was unremitting. Finally, she tore the first page off the printer.

"Okay, Mr. Heffelapfle," she said. "Question one."

I nodded.

"Is it true that you said you were going to punch Billy?"

I looked at my rep, then back at Patricia. "Yes," I said.

"Did it come out as an accident?"

I paused. "I don't know."

She looked up from her pad and pen. "You don't know."

"Don't know."

"So you would do it again, perhaps?"

"I don't know," I said. "I think that I would."

The Union person looked at me like I was crazy. I put my fingers in the air, like hand puppets.

"If Billy's fist hit Spencer," I said, "it is possible that he could knock Spencer out. If Spencer was knocked out, then it is possible that he would hit his head on the floor. Either from the punch, or the jolt on his head from hitting the floor - it is possible that the impact could have killed Spencer. It has happened before - deadly blows. Like in the Watts-Smith fight of 1823, Watts didn't mean to kill Smith. Or, just like in Rocky IV when Ivan Drago…"

"Please just say yes or no," Patricia said.

"Yes," I said, and then added, "I would do whatever would make Billy not hit Spencer with a possible life-threatening blow."

"Anything?" Patricia asked. "Would you tell him that you were going to shoot him if that came to mind?"

"Objection," the Union rep said. "You are baiting the witness."

"Maybe," I said. "Not likely. Depends on what I had for breakfast."

Patricia wrote this down. "Maybe he would shoot him."

I clutched onto my heart.

Shooting pains.

2.21.07

"I heard of a teacher who was fired last year because a kid lit a girl's hair on fire," one of the male teachers said over lunch.

"But that's not the teacher's fault," Hartman said.

"But it shows what kind of environment you have in your class," Schendel fired back.

"It shows what kind of environment the kid has at home and is *bringing* into my class."

"It doesn't matter," Schendel said.

"What do you mean it doesn't matter?"

"The district fired the teacher for *letting* that happen in her class."

I jumped in, "It's true that I would tell Billy again that I would punch him if he punched Spencer. Because if he hurt Spencer in my classroom, then it is my responsibility."

"See?" Schendel said to Hartman.

"And even if it's not," I said to Schendel, "I still feel like it is my responsibility."

"Is it though?" Hartman said, using his popsicle stick as a pointer. "No, the kids have got to take responsibility for their actions. It's not *you* the teacher, who is causing havoc. It is the kids. And so *they* should be sued. *They* should have their *parents* fired from *their* job of raising their out of control kid that is let loose in my classroom."

The science teacher, Dr. Cousteau jumped in. His voice was saturnine and deep. "Do you want to know what a person's greatest contribution to society is?"

"What?" I asked.

"Controlling their kid."

Once again, I felt a strange pain shoot down my arm.

149

2.22.07

So it was the middle of the night, and I couldn't sleep. This had been a common occurrence lately. At least the heart problems seemed to be waning. I looked at myself in the mirror. *What a terrible haircut.* I had stopped by Wal-Mart for a quick trim after work.

The barber was this bald Black guy who wore tiny silver framed glasses. It didn't seem like he should be cutting hair.

"I've been having chest pains, lately," I told him.

"Oh really?" he said.

It took him, like, an hour to see me. And he really seemed to have a chip on his shoulders. Snip, went his blades. Snip. Snip.

"I used to be a medic. And you know what?"

"What?" I asked.

"As soon as you feel chest pains go into your arm … and then your neck, run, don't walk to your cell phone and you dial 911 because you're about to have a stroke and the more you delay on this action the longer that it will take for the ambulance to reach you and get oxygen into an already deprived brain."

Snip. Snip.

The Applebee's is right across the street. I could get a haircut and then go over there and have a big slice of their apple pie, I thought. *Ouch! He just cut into part of my ear.*

"But I was wondering if it was heartburn?" I asked.

"That's the number one reason that people who have strokes tell me who didn't call 911 so they have to tell me by punching computer buttons with a straw in their mouths because they're paralyzed from the eyes down. 'Blink your eyes twice if you think I'm giving you a bad haircut.'"

I blinked my eyes twice.

Chapter 24

THE HEART ATTACK

2.28.07

So amidst all this, I got a speeding ticket for driving through a school zone at 55 miles per hour. And then, I forgot to pay the court.

But this time the cop pulled me over for not having proper stickers on my license.

"I'm a school teacher," I explained.

"Registration and insurance please."

"I seem to have forgotten them at home."

He looked at me from behind those silver mirror sunglasses. "That doesn't sound much like a school teacher to me, to not be paying his court fines. AND to be driving without insurance."

"Honestly, officer, it's because I'm putting so much time and energy into getting these kids off the streets and off drugs that I just forgot."

He rubbed his shoulder. "Well. Okay. But if you don't pay your bill by Tuesday, I will personally come and arrest you while you're teaching."

"Yes sir, thank you, sir."

I raced to the County Office. Such long lines. I grabbed a number. The sign said they were going to be closed Monday and Tuesday, so I needed to get the bill paid today. I was so tired that I fell asleep in my plastic chair. When I awoke, the court house was closing.

"I'm sorry," I told the lady behind the counter, as she pulled up all the warrants for my arrest. They were from speeding through the school zone and not paying the registration stickers. "I'm a school teacher. And the cop said he's going to personally arrest me if I don't pay the tickets, like right now."

This didn't seem to affect her.

I continued, "I have been so busy ... working with the kids. Making sure that they don't join gangs. What neighborhood do you live in? In my intense focus, saving one child at a time from meth addiction is a lengthy and uphill process that entails ..."

"Ignorance does not preclude you from the law, Mr. Heffelapfle," she said, pushing back her little glasses.

Once again, I felt those strange spasms in my heart. I could not imagine being in the classroom, teaching verb forms, as the kids went on one of their tirades.

"You're going to go to jail," I could see Billy saying.

"No I'm not," I would say.

"YES YOU ARE," the deep voice would say from behind me. I would turn around. There would be the cop, one hand on his hip. "Mr. Heffelapfle?"

"Yes?"

"We have a warrant for your arrest."

I would look at the police officer, stunned.

"You are going away for a very long time, Mr. Heffelapfle. A very long time."

The class would cheer as I am tazered.

I paid off the lady at the Court House, but only after having to borrow money from my dad once again to help pay off my tickets. ("I'm a failure...")

I went back to school.

3.17.07

Saint Patty's Day. And all the kids were trying to pinch me because I wasn't wearing green.

"He doesn't *have* to wear green, he's *Irish*," Anne Marie said, sticking up for me as usual. Poison Ivy came into my class wearing a giant leprechaun top hat, dark sunglasses, and a long flowing cape with silver sequins.

"I hate this fucking class," she said, sitting down, arms folded.

She looked so cute. I couldn't scold her for cussing. Ping. The fact that I ignored her must have, on some level, told her that it was okay to start stomping up and down and chanting.

"Leprechauns hate this school!" she shouted, quite literally breaking into song.

"They stay home drinking rum.
If I'm a leprechaun, I ask, 'why am I here?'
There seems to be no fucking rea-son."

The Leprechaun walked over to my overhead projector, and began ripping the transparencies off, one by one, making a real mess. I stared in awe, eating my donut, as she jumped up and down on today's lesson plan.

"I have magic powers, bitches!
I'm a badass! A leprechaun who smokes grass!
You can't stop me teacher! Buttfuck man!
Unless you bring me flowers, and even then
I'll fucking shoot you."

I just stared straight ahead. I was exhausted. My mind roamed on my crazy week. I couldn't believe that I had almost gotten arrested. *I've got to drive slower, man!* And then I thought of Patricia, eating her own excrement, like out of one of those Dairy Queen machines.

"Leprechauns don't kiss anyone's ass!
I hate this fucking class …yo yo! Break it down!"

The tension in my chest started up again. And this time, it was accompanied by a shooting pain down my left arm. I thought of the barber who warned me not to play it safe when it came to my health.

"Excuse me, kids, if you could keep it down for a moment. Sorry to interrupt the presentation," I said, dialing my cell phone. "Hello? 911?"

Poison Ivy stopped stomping on my lesson plans, and looked over. Then the entire room grew silent as all of the kids looked over at me.

"I think I'm about to have a heart attack," I whispered.

The kids stared at me, reading my lips.

The dispatcher's advice was pretty straight-forward. "You need to have an ambulance immediately."

Snip snip.

"What?"

"That's just my advice, Mr. Heffelnell," the lady said. "And as we're talking you're losing valuable seconds of oxygen that your brain might need to survive. So if you have an ambulance, they can do an EKG right there and bring the doctors to you."

"Okay," I said. "Do whatever you think is necessary. *But let's keep it quiet.*"

I hung up the phone.

The kids were all staring at me.

"What?" I said.

Ten minutes later, there were fire trucks in front of the school. Teachers were standing around and watching outside.

"Is this another fart bomb?" I heard one of them ask.

154

The medics cut off my shirt and began to cover me with little EKG stickers and dials. The students gathered around us, their eyes agape.

"I'm not finding anything Mr. Heffelwinger," the medic said. He was a younger kid who seemed new to the job. He took off a pair of latex gloves. "But my recommendation is that you go down to the hospital."

"Okay."

More medics came into my room, with a stretcher.

"I don't need to do that," I said, pointing to it.

"It's for your own safety," a nurse said.

All the teachers stood outside watching me being wheeled past them with tubes in my nose. I was picked up and placed inside the ambulance. Before I knew it, we were cruising out of the school parking lot, blue lights flashing.

Inside the ambulance the ambulance guy said, "You're awful young. Are you stressed out or something? What do you do?"

"I'm a teacher," I said, holding my chest.

They don't have room for you at the hospital anymore. All the rooms are taken. So it's like MASH. They put you out in the hallway. I saw some guy who was shot in the face. The blood spurted between his fingers. He was just a kid.

Hey, that looks like an 8th grader.

"Hello sir," I thought I heard.

"Kid Cassidy?"

The doctor then got in my face. He had my files in his hand. "Listen," he said. "You're only 26 years old, Mr. Heffelapfle. That's *nothing*. That's a *baby*. You don't have *time* to develop a heart condition. It takes until the age of about 40 to develop the degeneration from eating poorly, that kind of thing and you simply don't have the years needed to cause atrophy in your heart. I mean, what do you do?"

"I'm a teacher."

"Right. That means nothing to me, son."

"I told the ambulance driver ..."

"Twenty six years old is like 17 is like 12," he said, "is like a baby boy. A baby boy with degenerative heart atrophy who's having a stroke from too much stress ... It's *impossible*. But, considering the symptoms, the shooting pain in your left arm and in your chest ... that's textbook diagnosis of a precursor to a heart attack." He scratched his chin. "What website did you go to?"

"Excuse me?"

"Where did you look up this information about the pain?"

"I didn't."

"Because a lot of people use the internet now and they look up the information and then misdiagnose themselves."

"Well I didn't. This isn't some placebo affect. I'm not a hypochondriac."

"What's that? Placebo what? Huh? Never mind. Listen. Because your diagnosis and the words you chose are so specific, I'm going to have you stay here overnight because although the X-rays and EKG failed to provide evidence, I have a hunch that something is wrong with you. There's a little inner voice that I have learned to listen to, and been using it ever since I was a kid."

"Right," I said. "Me too."

He seemed perturbed. "Well since you're staying here you have to stay next to *him*," he said, pushing my wheel stroller next to this guy who was handcuffed to his bed.

The guy rolled over. A big scar was on his eye. "You dead?"

"No," I said.

"*You will be.*"

"I'll talk to you in a bit," the Doctor said.

On my left was some 500-pound guy and his crying wife. A doctor was talking over him about low antibodies. Then, over in the corner, there was a woman who is holding her stomach and screaming, "KILL ME!"

"Excuse me, Doctor," I said, "I would rather leave than stay here."

He looked at me, stunned. "I'm sorry?"

"I'm sure I'm okay," I said. "I would rather leave. I'm fine."

He just stared at me.

"Well," the doctor said, "because you are *disobeying* me, I'm going to have to have you sign a Death Waiver."

"I make my kids do that, too," I said.

"No, this is serious," he said. He pulled out a document which read "Coma", "Seizure", "Sudden Stoppage", and "Death".

"Sign here," he said. "Or you can't leave the hospital. It simply means that the hospital is not responsible for your actions from here on out, and that we warned you. Don't say we didn't *tell* you. Because we *did*."

"Where do I sign?" I said.

"So it's not our fault what happens in your classroom," he said. "If the kids act up, and you get tense again, don't say that the doctor didn't tell you that this would happen. Because we did. We warned you."

"Okay," I said, looking around at all the maniacs in his 'office'. It occurred to me that the doctor and I basically have the same job. Or is it that *all* professionals deal with this?

"A professional is someone who is able to deal with higher amounts of stress, and that's why they get paid more," my dad once told me. "Do me one favor and be one of those."

"Professional basically means 'job that deals with crazy people'," the doctor said. "And they actually put teachers in the same category as police officers and divorce court lawyers and what I do," he said, motioning to the screaming woman, the fat dying man next to me, the serial killer, and the kid who got shot in the face.

"Did you sign the Death Waiver?"

"Yeah."

"The exit's out that way."

I went back to school and kept teaching, but I was in a daze. When I went to my 8th grader meeting with the other teachers, Calista and JC, with the EKG heart stickers all over my arms and wires still hooked to my forehead, I just started crying.

"I have to go, I've had a really hard day," I said. Tears were coming out of my eyes.

"We've *all* had a hard day," JC said, but stopped short when she realized I was covered in computer cords.

"Jesus Mother of Mary."

She told me to stop working such long hours.

"Women can do that, men can't," she said to Calista. She looked at me, "If you continue at this pace, you're going to wind up in a clock tower offing people with a high powered rifle. When you do, make sure to tell me first so I can stay in my room."

I came home tonight. Fucking stressed only to call Margarita. It was ten at night. I sat there on my green blow up mattress, next to all of my books.

"Why do you keep calling?" she asked.

"Honestly it's because of my heart," I said. "And you're the only one I know. I had a rough day, you could say. So I'm a schmuck for calling, and I shouldn't. I just need to talk to someone."

"Well you don't deserve me. Don't call me to 'help' you anymore. My heart is hurt too."

"Good for you," I said.

"I'm better than you."

"Yes, stick up for yourself."

"So you have a nice life."

"Yes, get in the last word."

"Goodbye."

"Now hang up me," I said. "You go girl. Don't take that from me or anybody. You find somebody who loves you. Yes. Hang up. Now, before it's too late."

Click.

Chapter 25

THE HOUNDS OF
BASKETCASEVILLE

3.18.07

So the day started with Captain America when he pulled me out-side of my room.

"Pssst," he said. I went out into the hallway.

He whispered in my ear, "Keep this quiet, but they're monitoring you. Every time you send someone to the office -"

"What?"

"They're logging down every time some kid gives you a problem."

"So I can't send anyone out?"

"No, you can't," he said.

"No matter what?"

"No matter what. Don't do it. Keep the kids inside your class. No matter what happens."

I stared at Captain America for what felt like an eternity. I couldn't believe what he was telling me! If I can't send the kids out of my room when they're misbehaving ... well, they will tear me a new asshole. Is this what Patricia wanted?

I went back into my room, completely unable to continue teach-ing. I thought about starting up some crazy teacher revolution. ("How do you know it's not going to be *you* next? Or you, fatso? Or you or you or you?".)

Or about letting the kids do whatever they wanted. ("Call my class the sanctuary. Within these delicate borders, you may proceed as you wish. But take stock: the second an administrator walks through that invisible line," I would say, pointing at the door, "you are to attack.")

"Can I go to the bathroom?" some kid asked me.

"Yeah, I'm alright thanks for asking," I said. "You may speak amiably amongst yourselves."

Things were getting a little dizzy in here. Where were those antacids? My chest. I wanted to go into the secretary's office and give them a good scolding, too, for monitoring me. *"So now you have become that which you hate."*

I felt my jaw paroxysm with stress. My left arm weakened. A strange pain tore through my chin and face. A dull thumping sound rang in my ears followed by a queer feeling of impending doom.

But did it matter? I wasn't going to be here next year anyhow. Oh the pain. *I can't move.* Stuck in fifth period, now, with these little fucking beasts.

But the big lesson of today, before I discovered that I was being monitored, was that I have to act like I'm in a Shakespeare play instead of as Darth Vader to keep the students in line, for as long as we have the entropy at such a frenzied crescendo, it's important to be as strong as I can, as long as I can, before the class dissolves like a cube of ice.

The paralysis heightened as I realized that Patricia simply had it out for me. Then I thought of my dad, who explained to me the worst thing about Vietnam.

"There is nothing more terrifying than having some guy shooting at you, and you realize that it is you he is aiming at. You he is trying to kill," he said.

Patricia is a sociopath, and has no idea what it is like to teach 8th graders in our school, and so she lives in that safe haven as the outsider, where I'll confess I was once too, and from that angle in many ways I can't really blame her, because I have seen other 8th grade teachers who couldn't get control either. Man, and was I hard on them! So I have come to the conclusion that much like being shot at, teaching eighth grade is one of those experiences that you have to go through in order to fully comprehend.

3.19.07

We had another Teachers' Meeting today. It only proved to put my ass to sleep. When it was done, I went down to my classroom only to discover that Patricia was in the middle of a photo op. She had bought the latest Nikon digital camera and was using it to take pictures of my floor and file cabinets.

"Hey, what's up?" I asked, cheerfully.

She didn't answer me.

The janitor was with her.

"THIS IS UNACCEPTABLE," Patricia said, taking a picture of some crumpled paper on the floor. Then she found more scraps of paper, and made a little heap, and took pictures of those, too.

I watched her crawl on her hands and knees behind my desk.

She began opening up my drawers.

"Um uh ... don't do that," I began, but it was too late.

"AAAAAH!" she screamed.

She pulled out a bottle of yellow piss.

"That's lemonade," I said, quickly. "I bring it in by the truckload because it gets too hot in here."

She wrote this down. "Well we'll see what the labs have to say about that."

At this, the janitor began pulling bottle after bottle of urine from my desk.

"DON'T TOUCH IT," she said, putting on a pair of latex gloves. She pulled a pube off of one of the plastic Coke bottles and filed it inside of a manila folder.

"That's not mine, honestly I think somebody's trying to frame me," I said.

She winced. "Come to my office tomorrow Mr. Heffelapfle for another investigatory meeting."

And then, she marched out, evidence in hand. I looked over at the janitor.

"So what are your plans for the weekend?" I asked.

"I just can't believe the politics here," she said. "Well I'll talk to you later."

"Aren't you going to dump the trash cans?"

"No, I'm afraid Patricia has strict orders for me not to dump your trash anymore."

"Isn't that a health violation? What are we going to do, just let it pile up until it turns into the dump?"

"I'm sorry, Mr. Heffelapfle. I'm sorry."

I'll admit that I couldn't sleep last night ... couldn't stop thinking abut tomorrow's big war with Patricia. I tossed and turned all night.

Then, the next day, bright and early, I found myself in the meeting.

3.20.07

"Why didn't you clean up your room like was ordered?" Patricia said, twisting her pencil.

"Because of grade day, I got messy. A lot of teachers were messier than me."

"But we're focusing on *you*, Mr. Heffelapfle."

"I forgot. You need to build your case," I said. "But *you* keep forgetting that *I* am a *new* teacher."

"I haven't forgotten anything."

We stared at each other over her desk. Finally, I continued, "My understanding is that teaching for first year teachers is extremely difficult. Add to this the fact that we are literally the *worst* middle school in the district. Ask me what happened to my classroom, and I'll tell you that the worst kids in all of Las Vegas – 150 of them - just barged through my class. And until you have actually taught 8th graders here at this school, I think that it's impossible to understand what we, as 8th grade teachers go through."

"I know what you go through."

"Have you taught 8th grade for a title one at-risk lower socioeconomic ..."

"This is not about *me*," she interrupted. "It is about *you. You* are on trial here."

"Trial? We are on trial?"

"I don't have to put up with this."

"Listen. Listen. Patricia," I said, aggressively. *"Listen."*

She looked at me. Flushed red.

"Is this what you want?" I unbuckled my pants. "IS THIS WHAT YOU WANT?"

I laid my cock on the desk.

"DOES THE SMELL OF MY PISS DRIVE YOU CRAZY, BITCH? THAT'S WHY YOU WERE ON YOUR HANDS AND KNEES, TAKING PICTURES. THAT'S WHY YOU WERE WATCHING ME, ALWAYS RIGHT BEFORE I WENT TO THE BATHROOM. IT WAS BECAUSE YOU WANTED IN. YOU WANTED IN TO WATCH ME TAKE A SHIT DIDN'T YOU? I COULD HEAR YOU, CLAWING AT THE DOOR TRYING TO GET IN."

I'll admit that this was a big gamble on my part. But I was certainly forcing her to decide, right there in her office. Was it going to be ME? Or that aged principal who lied about fighting in the war?

"Okay," she said.

"Okay," I nodded. "You know Hitler enjoyed getting peed on. It's the only way he could get off."

"He was a distant relative of mine," she said, getting on her hands and knees.

"Open your mouth, bitch."

And I just released it.

Like I had a million times before, camping. Like I had a million times before, on Alexandria, and behind my teacher's desk when no one was looking.

In the midst of it, her hand fell upon the intercom button.

All the teachers could hear her calling my name from the loud speaker.

"Mr. Heffelapfle! OH! MR. HEFFELAPFLLLLLE!"

I woke up.

Soaked in sweat.

Sleeping behind my desk.

Another nightmare. I reached for a water bottle and then immediately spat it up. I had drunk my piss on accident again.

I went down to JC's room. She seemed really upset over something.

"I'm going to kill that bitch," JC said. I wanted to ask her if she meant Patricia, but who else could she be talking about? There was only one bitch in the school.

"She's all *on* me about my lesson plans not being turn in," she said. "I turned in the fuckin' lesson plans to her dumb, new secretary."

"I did too," I said. "Apparently she's losing them."

"How did your meeting go? Your ...," and then, she laughed, "your 300th investigation?"

"It went well. I explained that it was grade day, the busiest day of the year, and she said okay. Then I went home and had a really strange dream of her and me getting it on."

"Eww."

"The lab reports of the pee turned up inconclusive unless they get blood samples from me and I'm not giving them shit."

"I'm going to punch her in the face," JC said. "I've never seen a Jewish-Latino with that fuckin' nose of hers. Don't repeat what I'm saying, because it's racist."

"Okay, I won't."

"My mother was just like that bitch," she continued. "Could never say anything nice. But see the thing was, was that she had my *father* to balance her out. Patricia ain't got no *father*... well, they say what doesn't kill you makes you stronger, and if *that's* the case you must be Popeye the Sailor Man, Leo. You don't have muscles, you've got MUS-CLES."

Chapter 26

MY PINK FAG SHIRT

3.23.07

In case you have forgotten what it's like to be in the 8th grade, they are obsessed with homosexuals. And this is annoying because it shows no class. On the other hand, these are kids. And no one has ever explained to them why FAG is their favorite word.

"Get off my desk," I said to Maria. I turned to the class. "Can anybody tell me what the origin of 'fag' is?"

I let Maria and her little friends get too close behind my desk, lately. So now they were sitting on it, trying to change their grades in my computer, and poking me.

"Stop it. This is annoying. Sit down. Leave me alone. Now. Back in the days when they would have witch hunts …" I began, pushing Maria toward her desk, "they would actually burn people alive for being homosexuals."

"What's a homosexual?" someone asked.

"It's what you would call a fag," I said.

Maria was back up at my desk. This was irritating. I didn't want to be one of those teachers that liked the girls better than the boys. I hated those teachers when I was back in school. It was usually the gym teacher who taught math. So I had to stop this right now.

"GET AWAY FROM ME SIRENS!" I roared. I took a drink from my purified water container. "Faggots are actually just bundles of sticks, but back in puritan days, the sticks would run out…"

Jesus, Maria was on my computer.

I wiped off my grizzled face. "Maria, sit down. In your chair. Are we going to have another 'episode'? Sit down. Good. When we're in my class, I'm your master, and you're a no-good monkey."

Maybe I needed to buy a whistle. That would get her attention. Blow it in her ear every time she didn't listen to me. Wind up with a class of deaf kids.

"They would actually throw the gay people on top of the fire in place of kids," I said. "I mean, in place of sticks. So just think about that the next time you are using that word."

"Why is it so important to you," Linda asked. "Is it because *you* are gay?"

"I don't know if I'm gay," I said. "The point is, hate is bad. Here, let me show you some pictures of the bonobo monkeys."

I *had* been thinking for quite some time that boundaries must be established with these three nymphets – who have been getting closer and closer. *And the closer they get, the less post-it notes I have.*

Maria raised her hand.

"Yes, Maria?" I asked. "This better have to do with homosexuals."

"Can I go to Mr. Hartman's?"

Her friend jumped in. "Yes, can we?"

"Why?"

It suddenly occurred to me, that these little girls were wearing the skimpiest outfits possible. Why do they make these? Is this unethical? Hm. Was it somehow playing on my subconscious? *Oh my God, am I slowly turning into a pedophile? That's kind of hot. No. How long has it been since I saw a real woman?*

No. Jesus Christ.

You only see these kids, you are becoming one of them. Distortions of reality.

It's only because Maria reminds you of Kim, I thought. What a mind-fuck. *I shouldn't be a teacher.* I'm a monster of some sort. *No. These feelings are natural. It's your Id. Watch them, let them pass.*

"Yeah, sure," I said. "Whatever. Go to his class, if he gives you more attention."

Brita water ran down my beard.

This is happening because it was now springtime. The girls were filled with estrogen, and releasing large amounts of pheromones into the air. *Yeah, that's it. It's mating season. And I'm just picking up on it, that's all. They're brainwashing you. The chemicals are floating in the air, like pollen.*

I wrote them a pass, one by one.

Someone's perky breast was on my back.

"Maria, back up," I said. "And put some clothes on. Does your mother know you're dressed like this? When you're older, you'll learn there are words for women who dress like you are."

I remember going to a school dance with Hartman. And at it, we just stood there, chaperoning, watching all of our students - these adolescent little girls, smashing their asses into each as the rave music played, euphorically.

"I don't pay attention to this," he said.

"Neither do I," I said.

I looked over at Mr. Schendel.

He gave me a queer thumbs-up sign.

There was something about him that really bothered me.

As the door shut to my room, and Maria left for Hartman's, I couldn't help but to reflect on the fact that even a 13-year-old girl could manipulate me. This had to have something to do with my mom.

You're so far away, I miss you, Leo, I imagined her saying. My eyes welled up with tears. *I miss you, too.*

While connecting to the telekinetic grid, I did not notice that my star student, Shane, a flaming homosexual, was now taping up pictures of my face. There was my face, on the clock, ceiling, and walls.

"That's me!" I shouted, pointing. "Shane! What are you doing?"

"I'm just taping your picture up onto the clock, Mister. I think we should have your picture up everywhere, throughout the school."

"That's not a bad idea. But this is a poor shot of me."

"No it's not. It's the one of you in your pink fag shirt."

"Don't say that word. Remember what we just talked about? Remember who you are. Remember who you come from - the monkeys."

"This is a good picture of you, sir," Shane said. "It's the one where you subconsciously try to teach the kids that homophobia is wrong, and that it's okay to wear pink, and thereby, be a faggot."

I thought about this.

"And you're saying these pictures will be everywhere?"

"Yes, sir."

"Well I guess you can say that word, but only around me. This might be like Black people using the 'n-word'. An instant A for effort. You just solidified an A in my room, my lad. Do your parents know about your gifts?"

He had about 500 pictures of me in his backpack.

As much as I was honored, another part of me had a revelation. *This was psycho.* And, being late in the day, after much coffee, I appeared to be acting psycho, too.

"Did you just run these off at Kinko's?" I asked.

He grabbed some extra tape off my desk. "Excuse me, sir. We'll need pictures of you hanging off the overhead lights."

"Shane, now, not to be rude, but would you mind telling me where you got all these pictures of me?"

"From Ricardo, mister."

Ricardo.

Ricardo was a student that used to be good, that went bad. 2nd period. He was a larger student, six feet tall, abnormally protruding around the shoulders and neck area. He was also into rhyming. I really liked him at first. But then, something happened as second period rolled around. *A metamorphosis.* Part of me thought it was puberty. You know, testosterone. But then I thought something else. Yes. He was influenced by Poison Ivy, the Terrible. Now he was one of those kids that refused to sit down in his seat. And he was throwing things at me with those large gorilla arms.

Ask him to be quiet and he'd say, "Why? Why?"

"Because I said to."

"Why?"

"Because those are the rules."

"Why?"

"Because the administration created them back in the early 20th century when they were creating the school system."

"Why?"

"Because we decided children must be educated."

"Why?"

"Because kids were running amok and we needed social order."

"Why?"

"Because you might wind up thinking for yourselves if you are not contained."

"Why?"

"Because the government is scared of people who have time on their hands."

"Why?"

"Because you might take it over."

"Why?"

"Because you might have a better way to run things."

"Why?"

"Because you have a Will to Power."

"Why?"

"Because all creatures have it."

"Why?"

"Because you need it to survive."

"Why?"

"Because life wants to live."

"Why?"

"Perhaps so it can observe the universe."

"Why?"

"Because space is lonely."

"Why?"

"God got bored."

"Why?"

"Because wouldn't you be if you were all alone?"

"Why?"

"So he or she blew himself up in this giant big bang."

"Why?"

"And we're now just shard fragments."

"Why?"

"Self-referential computer patterns."

"Why?"

"Have you ever taken lysergic acid?"

"Why?"

"No, you're too young."

"Why?"

"It doesn't matter."

"Why?"

"Well, because you and I are stuck."

"Why?"

"Here in this system."

"Why?"

"And if karma or reincarnation is real, we're both screwed."

"Why?"

"Did you know the animals in those slaughter houses are actually living in a perpetual holocaust?"

"Why?"

"And you and I did nothing to save them."

"Why?"

"Maybe in another dimension we were once those animals."

"Why?"

"And maybe we said, 'God if you make me human, I will change this travesty.'"

"Why?"

"And now we aren't doing anything about it."

"Why?"

"We're just like everyone else."

"Why?"

"Like drops from a waterfall."

"Why?"

"All parts of the same waterfall."

"Why?"

"Well not me, bubba. Have you ever seen 'The Cove'?"

"Why?"

"I'm going to kill those people who kill those dolphins."

"Why?"

"Never mind, I've said too much."

"Why?"

"I'll wait until I'm an old man, though."

"Why?"

"Sit down. I don't want to play anymore."

"Why?"

"We're holding up the class."

"Why?"

"Well, because you won't stop talking."

"Why?"

"Sit down."

"Why?"

"Now."

"Why? Why? Why? Why? Why? Why? Why? Why? Why? Why? Why? Why? Why? Why? Why? Why? Why? Why? Why? Why? Why? Why? Why? Why? Why? Why? Why? Why? Why? Why? Why? Why? Why? Why? Why? Why? Why? Why? Why? Why? Why? Why? Why? Why? Why? Why?"

Fucking infuriating. Like a robot malfunction.

I stood in front of the class, holding my pictures. "So to reiterate, when these faggots or sticks would run out," I said, "they would actually *throw* the gay people on top of the fire in place of the kids."

"Why?" asked Ricardo.

"I'm not going to go round and round with you," I said.

"Why?"

I ignored him. It was my only defense. Like a bug, playing dead. I could threaten him, when we were alone. Tell him I would beat his ass. Pull out Vader. But honestly, I couldn't stand to hear "Why?" again.

Moments later, after I had made Shane sit back down, there was a knock on the door. It was Mr. Hartman.

"Did you get my gift?" I asked.

"No. Gift? What?" He was holding a picture of me in my pink shirt. "Did you send me your picture?"

"No," I said.

"Did you write this?" He turned the picture over. On the back of it was a note that read:

Hi dude
I'm siting hear so horny
Want to come over and
Eat me.
I'm gay.
Peace out.
XOXO Mr Hefferfu

"I didn't write that," I said, raising two Boy Scout fingers in the air. But I could see that part of him didn't believe me.

"No really, I didn't," I said.

He didn't respond.

"Who gave you the note?"

"Maria," he said.

I looked at Maria, who was hiding behind him.

I threw my arms in the air. "I let you go out of my class, to be nice, for the first time ever, and this is how you treat me?"

She clinched her face at my words. Then she muttered, "They put me up to it."

"Who did?"

She pointed at Shane. He was gluing the television set with pictures of my face.

"We're watching Mr. H," Shane said. "All the channels are the Mr. H Show."

Hartman looked at me, like I should stop this.

"No, he's special," I said to him.

177

"He's a fag," Maria said.

I then looked at her like I was going to kill her. "What did I teach you today?"

She turned red.

"I mean … fags are put on fires. Shane is a homosexual, which is okay," she said. "It's okay to be a homosexual."

I looked at Hartman, amazed.

"Is everyday like this?" he asked.

"No," I said. "They learned something today."

3.27.07

Just to get my mind off of work, sometimes I would do crazy things. One time I went on the rollercoaster at the "New York New York." This is a coaster that wraps all the way around one of those mini skyscrapers. It's kind of small. But it's always been in the back of my mind.

So I go there, after work, again, and see some kid in line, who's got bleached blonde hair, a Sid Vicious coat with patches of different punk bands, and a goatee.

"This isn't scary is it?" I asked him.

He began to talk with an English accent. "No this isn't scary. I rode on it with my little cousin last year."

"Good deal," I said.

We waited in line.

Next thing I know, I'm on the ride and those big yellow clamps come down. I look at him and smile. Suddenly, things began to pick up. We race around the corner, and I see something that takes my breath away. The ride appears to shoot straight into the air, into some interminable atmosphere of earth. Almost like it planned to take us into the clouds. Or heaven. I couldn't see where it ended.

"You know when I told you that this ride isn't scary?" the kid said.

"Yeah?"

"I take it back."

We soared into the ionosphere at such a frenzied rate that I suddenly thought, *I might not be able to survive the ride.* You know, because of my heart. And once you start something like this, you can't turn around. It's a one-way ticket. You're clamped in by these giant yellow steel bars.

I felt like Superman who had been encaged by Dr. Doom.

"Get me out of here," I tried to mouth.

I began to struggle.

Every year people die on rides like these. It's rare. But on occasion, someone has a fucking heart attack.

"Get me out of here," I tried to mouth, again.

I don't know if I'll survive this.

"WHAT?" the kid yelled back at me.

"GET ME OUT OF HERE!"

I had to think, and quick! How do I survive? Darth Vader? I haven't tried Luke, yet! No. That's fucking stupid! Pretend like I'm on a spaceship? Zooming through the universe? Time to attack the rebel hull! No! Think, man! And I suddenly realized there's one emotion that is very similar to falling. And that's sex. Dopamine and adrenaline get released in the reaction-response rate to orgasm – a sensation which is very much like falling. So if I just pretended that I was having sex, really wild sex, I might survive.

As we reached the top, I closed my eyes, and thought of Alexandria.

When the ride is done, they show you your picture right before you freefall 180-feet off a steel cliff. Everyone had these looks like they were going to die. Not me, though. I was fainting in ecstasy. Thank god for those steel clamps.

They say that if you think of something with all of your emotions, you can attract it into your life. Well, soon after riding the roller coaster, I met my Las Vegas, Nevada love.

You see, another one of the crazy things I would do to get my mind off Patricia was to visit poetry readings. These old fogies at the Coffee Shack would get up, lumber over to the podium, and read "Howl". Each syllable, boisterously staccato'ed out like in morse code. And I would try to imbibe the words, thinking it might help my lyrics for my songs. I don't know if it helped.

Well, one week, I forgot one of my books there – and when I came back the next week, there was this woman there in the corner of "The Shack" reading it, surrounded by her girlfriends.

"Hey," I said, coming up to her. "You know, I actually left that here, last week ... But you don't have to stop reading it, now."

She had short brown hair and this amazing smile.

"You read physics?" she asked me.

"Yeah."

"Do you like fractals?"

"What's a fractal?"

"Oh my god, you don't know what a fractal is?"

And thus began our mutual amazement because no one in Vegas: A. Reads, or B. Reads physics. So she started teaching me about fractals and I started giving her lectures on mythology, the hero's journey, and Joseph Campbell.

We traded numbers.

CALL ME
DESTINY 702-393 ...

Chapter 27

CANDY

3.30.07

At the end of the day, I would often find myself crawling on my hands and knees, cleaning up the litter that the kids had left behind. I tried to make the kids do it, but if they couldn't lift a pencil, how were they supposed to lift a candy wrapper?

So to help me get the kids to clean the floor, Mr. and Mrs. Fiehr went out and bought me candy from Big-Mart. One of those really big bags filled with every type of candy imaginable.

"I don't know why it works, it just does in class. They'll do any-thing for candy," she said.

"Well geez, thank you, Anne Marie," I said.

And she was right. I took their five dollar bag of candy and hid it inside my desk. And then, after each class period I would offer it to the good kids who helped me clean my floor. At first I didn't believe that this would work. *Like they could actually get paid off by candy*, I smirked. *I think we're beyond that. These kids are more like terrorists. They're going to want a million dollars and a Cessna to Israel.* But, much to my surprise, it was like feeding tuna to a dolphin.

And I mean *anything, man.*

They would do *anything* for the candy. Including, as they proved, *relieve* me of the giant bag when I wasn't looking.

"Where's my fucking candy?" I said, after sixth period had ended.

My desk drawer was empty. Five dollars down the drain. Oh great. And I thought I almost caught the vandal. But see, this guy's heist was the perfect crime. He somehow got into my desk when I wasn't looking. I didn't know that there even *was* a robbery until I heard Cassandra screaming after class.

"EDDIE STOLE IT! EDDIEEE!"

"Where? Where?" I asked. "What?"

I ran past her, outside my class, and by the purple pole. I looked around. Kids were everywhere, like sea birds. I couldn't see through the fray.

And then I saw him.

"Eddie! STOP!" I shouted.

There. Through the crowd. The short bald kid.

"EDDIE!"

He stopped in his tracks, and turned around slowly, with his hands in the air.

I ran over to him.

"Where's the candy, Eddie?" I said, patting him down.

He looked at me in disbelief. "What are you talking about? What do you mean? I don't know. What candies are these?"

"You know what candies!"

But then again: Eddie? Pull a fast one on me? He couldn't have! He's too stupid. Besides, the five dollar bag is gigantic. And he obviously wasn't holding onto it. It would have been bulging through his clothing.

"Never mind," I said. "You may go."

When I went back into my room, I noticed that the kids decided to mix heist with malice by spitting all over my chairs. Considering that Hep-C can live in spit for 10 days, I decided not to clean it up. Let all the kids get infected.

That's what you get for stealing my candy.

The next day I found the empty candy bag. Actually, a student found it because I saw her walking out the door with it on her head. *Taunting me with it.*

"Stop! Cassandra!" I couldn't believe my eyes. "What is that on your head?"

"It's your candy bag, mister," she said. "There used to be candy in it. There's no candy in it now."

I felt my face turning red.

Fucking candy.

The next period of the day was Eddie's. I couldn't wait for class to get over. And of course, all the kids were acting freaking bananas. I don't know how come I put up with this, I thought. And then I remembered, I don't. I apparently don't have any choice. I'm powerless. I try to stop it and it doesn't work. I've tried a million different methods.

But fuck the class.

Find the candy.

As soon as that bell rings I stop him at the door. I tell him we're going to have an investigatory meeting. He thinks I'm joking at first. When we go back inside my class, and I tell him to sit down, he sees I'm not. I stare at him for at least a minute before I begin the pressure cooker.

I turn off the lights and point my desk lamp at him. Light up a cigarette.

His bald little face looks at me in the dark.

"Okay, 'Eddie'," I say. "Question number one: Why did you take my candy?"

"What? What Mister?" he says. "I didn't take your candies!"

He holds his hands up in the air. "Mister!" he says. "How could I? How could I fit them into my pocket if they weren't in their bag?"

"What did you say?" I fire back.

And at this, he covers his mouth.

I smile. "That was information that only the robber and I know, Eddie. Stay here. Stay right here."

I get up and go next door to find Anne Marie. I can't find her anywhere. Her room smells like the sulfur chloride the Germans would use when they would kill the French and Belgians in WWI. I put my shirt up to my face and run out into the hallway. Finally, I find her out by the water fountain. She's snickering with the other teachers about something.

"OH YES," she is saying. "And then he only managed to have the candy for one period before they took it away from him."

"What an idiot," one of the teachers says.

And then Anne Marie sees me walking up. "Oh! Uh … Hi Mr. Heffelapfle. We were just talking about your classroom management skills."

They all snicker.

"Yeah, well," I say, "I actually let the student pull the heist off, to test him. You've got to catch them early. What's candy today is carjacking tomorrow."

"What? You caught him?"

"I did."

"Who did it?" she said, gasping.

"Follow me."

Of course Eddie wasn't in my room when we went back. So we had to wait until the next day to set up a series of traps involving more candy that I won't get into. The bottom line is this: We grabbed Eddie as he was walking by my room, and pulled him in for an inquisition.

"What the …" he stammered.

"WHERE ARE THEY? *Just tell me*," Anne Marie screamed. "If you tell me you did it Eddie, you're not in trouble."

"I don't have the candies …"

"Eddie," she repeated, "you don't have to lie to me."

"I KNOW YOU DID IT," I shouted.

He began to cry under our questioning. *"I don't have candies ..."*

"I *know* you know who took it," Anne Marie said. "TELL US!"

"Tell Anne Marie what you told ME!" I screamed.

"What?" he said.

"That you knew the candy wasn't in the bag!"

His eyes widened – large, like gumballs.

"You KNEW the candy wasn't in the bag?" her voice pounded.

"NO!" he yelled. The tears really began to come on.

"That's enough to *incriminate* you right there," she said. "I should take you down to the office right now -."

"For a cavity search," I said.

His jaw dropped. "I didn't take the candies!"

You would think that if there was one person on this planet who could teach him how to say candy and not candies it would be either his parents or me, because I'm his English teacher. But since he stole my candy I decided I would let him continue to keep speaking in bad grammar for the rest of his life.

"Where are the *candies*, Eddie? Just tell me where the candies is."

3.31.07

After 'Eddie' betrayed me, I stopped feeding the kids candy. I didn't feel that they deserved it anymore. Maybe I was overreacting to all of this. Maybe I got caught up there for a little bit. Maybe this wasn't so important in the larger scheme, I thought, smiling. I stared at my water. It was getting late. Cassandra, one of the teacher's pets, was attempting to grade some papers for me.

In exchange, she would of course, want candy.

I became somewhat serious, which was appropriate.

"No, Cassandra," I said. "After what happened ... I ... can't go back. The candy debacle got out of control."

"But mister, you owe me something for getting an A on my test. At least an apple Jolly Ranchers. Everybody else in the class failed."

"No. Sit down," I snapped. "No."

She wasn't used to me snapping like this. Maybe at other kids, but never at her. Her mouth dropped, like she was about to say something. For a second she held back. But then unable to restrain herself, she just let it go. "Oh Mister, I forgot to tell you."

"What?"

"I ... had the most terrible dream with you in it."

"Oh yeah?" I opened up a newspaper. "What happened?"

A sick smile came across her face. Then it faded away. "You went crazy, and you were going to kill me and the class."

I looked up. "Oh?"

"Yes," she said.

She played with the little buttons and patches on her shirt as she talked to me. Some had little bright yellow smiley-faces on them. Others had frowns. And still others seemed to be crying.

"We all drove you to it," she said. "You had a sword in your hand, and you put chains on all the door handles so we couldn't get out. Then you called up your mom and dad on your cell phone, and told them to call 9-1-1 because all your kids were going to die."

I opened my desk drawer and reached into my new candy bag. The secret candy bag. I took out a Tootsie Roll and put it in her hand.

"More," I said.

"Then you started slicing up the kids but some of us got away. You chased us to your apartment and were trying to hack your way through the door."

She opened up the Tootsie Roll.

"Well," I said. "There's a flaw in the story. My apartment is miles from here."

"You would never do that to us, would you, Mister?" she asked.

I shook my head. "Well it sounds like you're not only a poor student, but a prophet as well."

"Can I get more candy?"

"No," I said. "Sit *down.*"

4.1.07

But who cares about candy when you're in love.

Destiny invited me over to her house for dinner and I gave her a juniper plant from Trader Joe's at the front door, along with a giant watermelon, cantaloupe, and large hug.

She cooked up a homemade vegetarian entrée and for the first time since I had been in Vegas, I actually felt really alive. She didn't even live in Vegas. She lived right outside it, in a tiny suburb. So her energy wasn't perverted. Well not that much.

"So what's it like teaching middle school?" she asked.

"Well it's um ..."

But before I could continue, she said, "You're so lucky. Those kids need good teachers like you. Because these kids, nowadays, have been virtually abandoned by their parents. And I know what that's like."

"You do?"

"Oh yeah. I've been through hell and back. But I'm okay, now."

"Right. Well these kids do need a leader. That's for sure."

After eating, she led me into her bedroom. She showed me her books on kundalini and tantric yoga, which I said were two of my loves. "But I don't have any time to pursue them," I said, "because all my energy seems to have been mysteriously diverted."

She thought she could help with that, and so we did yoga on her bed and then fell asleep in each other's arms. She woke up to me grinding into her like an attack dog.

"What are you doing?" she asked.

"Huh? Oh, nothing," I said.

"I'm not going to have sex with you."

We went into the kitchen to get a drink of water.

"Okay, I'm just going to say it," I said. "I'm like a Navy Seals Commando."

She just stared back at me, wearing nothing but her underwear and t-shirt. She took a drink from her glass of water. Her lips were now covered with a filmy coat of gloss.

"And Mother Nature has given me the impossible task of getting my sperm into your vagina," I said. "The latest research suggests that sperm are smart, not dumb, as you might think. They can actually count how much calcium is concentrated in their environment, like a mathematician."

My mouth was just running off a series of excuses.

"And because I haven't jerked off for four days," I said, leaning in, "there's a plethora of this 'smart sperm' – and I don't want them to die. I want them to live. I want *us* to live."

"Whoa," she said.

"What?"

"You haven't masturbated for four days for me?"

I nodded.

She bit her finger.

Chapter 28

THE LIBRARIAN

4.3.07

When you're in love, you can get in fights, and you don't really care. Like just a second ago, frickin' moments ago, I had it out with the librarian. She's so cocky. Just because she's good looking she thinks she can be a bitch.

"I don't know why I should let you check out books for your class," she said, bending over a shelf. She had this really long blonde hair that extended down to her waist. I imagined her riding on top of a horse, naked along the ocean.

But then I remembered that I was with Destiny and so I had to be loyal, now.

"Hello? Mr. Heffelapfle?" she said, waving her hand in front of my face. "Do you actually think that they are going to read them?"

Loyal.

"Some might," I said. "But regardless they should have the opportunity to read."

"Oh," she said. She changed her tone, sarcastically. "Excuse me for venting, here, Mr. Heffernan, but they destroyed half of your last class set. And now you want more? They don't return their books, and now you want more? Yours is the only class that comes in and doesn't check out books."

Now I saw her on a black horse covered in mud whipping her slaves. I didn't want to be one of her slaves if I was taken.

"Okay," I said. "First point, they did destroy my first class set. And I'm genuinely sorry about that."

"No you're not. You don't care."

"That's not true. I do care."

"No you don't."

"Yes I do. And about them returning their books, I'm sorry. But I tell them to return their books. I give them forms that say to return their books. I yell at them to return their books. What am I supposed to do, follow them home? Put a gun up to their head?"

"No, but don't reward them and tell them they can have these books."

"Well I feel like even though they made the mistake and didn't return their other books they should still have the opportunity to read."

"Well make them read your English books down in your English storage room. You guys have textbooks."

"Have you seen those? That's like reading a car manual. I wouldn't wish that on my worst enemy, much less these kids. I wouldn't make Hitler read that tripe."

"Well," she said. Her gesture broke off to signify that I was in no position to question the assigned teaching literature. Then she said in a slow, dry and pained tone, "I'll give you the books … but I just thought you should know that your disorganized shamble of a class has been unruly all year, comes into my library, never checks anything out, and now you want to hand-feed them dessert and it makes me sick."

"Don't judge until you have taught 8th-graders at this school."

"I have. Eight years ago I taught 8th-graders."

"Well the socio-dynamics have changed since then."

"What does that mean? They're the same kids."

"No they're not," I said. "Back then, they were mostly African Americans. And now, 90 percent of them are Latinos."

"Which means what?"

"My understanding is that the Black kids were more aggressive and that their parents would 'whoop their asses' more if they didn't behave and get good grades. That's right, 'whoop their asses.'"

She raised an eyebrow.

"The Latinos, on a cultural level, appear to be more apathetic and misbehaved. That's just what all the teachers say. I have Latino kids, you *had* Black kids."

"Oh please, Mr. Hefferniple. You don't know how to control your kids. Stop making excuses. Pulling the race card."

"Pulling the *cultural* card. Latinos come here, half my kids don't know the language. And they don't value Western education in the same way. Why should they get an education when they can go work in the casinos for as much money as someone who has a Master's degree? The Black kids appear to value western education more on a stereotypical level, and their parents are *more* strict generally speaking, again. Besides, half of these Latino parents who I have to deal with aren't even home. They're just trying to survive. I mean, after they've finished navigating the obstacle course just to get into the United States, the only job they can get is working all night in the casinos, again. So most my kids have no parents until they're unleashed in my class. So don't judge until you have taught *Latino* 8th-graders at this school."

"Mr. Heffelapfle, we're obviously not going to agree on this point."

"Mrs. Colter, we can agree on one thing: I have decided that I don't want your stupid books. You can have'em. What are you doing with all these books? Nothing. Never met a librarian who forgets the kids. You should read 'Scrooge' by Charles Dickens."

She looked at me like I was crazy. "No," she said. "You're going to get them."

"No I'm not."

"Yes you are. Why would you be so affected by what I say."

"*Because you're so beautiful.*"

She looked up from behind the returned bookstand, (which was empty).

"It's true," I said. "And that's why I'm not taking your books."

"No you are."

"No I'm not."

"You have no choice."

"Yes I do."

"You're taking them, now."

"No," I said, walking out. "You can't make me."

When I went back to my room, I got on my cell phone and called my mom and dad and started crying.

"Well I'm concerned about the Latino situation, too," my dad said, up there in Montana. "We might have a serious situation on our hands. If the Latinos continue to propagate at the rate they are, then who knows what will happen."

"That's what I tried to tell her, Dad."

"Do you know the statistics for how many people in the LA basin speak English? It's not high. Something like 90 percent of them speak Spanish. The whites are the minority. And quite frankly, if you look at California, Texas, and Arizona, they believe that those lands were taken from them. And rightfully so. None of those treaties held. Look at the Treaty of Guadalupe."

"Right."

"You know, Leo, if they were able to somehow organize, we would have another Civil War on our hands."

"That's what I tried to tell her Dad. And that's why the 8th graders are out of control. Here put Mom on the phone."

I heard my mom coming to the phone. It took her a long time to get there. She was getting older. I didn't like not being there. I told her everything that had happened.

"... And then the librarian told me not to check out her books," I said.

I wiped away my tears.

"Can I have money?"

Chapter 29

SPRING BREAK

4.5.07

Finally. Two weeks of pure bliss. Spring break. Seriously, it's the only thing that got me through. And it came out of nowhere.

When I went home after the librarian fight, and saw my apartment in desiccated shambles, I wondered if I was slowly going crazy. But in these two weeks, I'd clean it all up and get a fresh start. I even found a fish aquarium out by the trash. Maybe I'd get some fish. Put some food out in the cat dish for those starving cats I saw roaming around. No more of this crazy business.

Heck, I could spend two weeks playing music, finding myself again. "Oh yeah, I'm a musician," I said, looking into the mirror. Were those gray hairs growing out of my ears? Maybe I could go up to Montana. Yes. That would be grand! Clean up tomorrow. Make love to Destiny. And go to bed tonight – alone, though – yes – I needed this "me" time to relax for the first time in my life. Put on those new pillowcases.

Before I knew it, I was conked out. Had strange dreams. They were about someone who was beating on a slab of wood. I opened an eyelid. *No, that's somebody at the door.*

I looked at my clock. 3:30 in the morning.

I fell back asleep.

But then I woke up again, to that knocking sound. It was about 5:30. I figured I would answer it.

I get up, go down the hallway, and poke my eye through the peep-hole. I flip the outside light on, but I can't see who is out there because we forgot to change the light bulb. So all I see is this silhouette.

"Who's there?" I say.

"It's me, Colin," a voice says back.

Now I know what Colin's voice sounds like. And this isn't my roommate. MY Colin has a very distinctive voice. I think this is because he plays saxophone, and you know how a person can take on the quali-ties of the instrument they play? Just like anything else? Well my Colin sounds like an alto saxophone with just the right amount of reed. This new Colin didn't sound like that.

"Yeah - it's me, Colin," he says. "Let me in."

I freeze.

Before I can answer, he says, "Oh wait! Dude! Don't open the door! Before you do anything, you've got to look out the balcony win-dow and see what's going on over the city of Las Vegas!"

Now let me explain how my apartment is positioned: I'm on the second floor and there is a flight of stairs leading up to the door. These same stairs lead down to the front of the apartment, where there is a large grassy knoll. In front of the knoll is a large 10 foot wall. My balcony looks over this grass, facing the wall, and facing the city of Las Vegas. From up on the balcony you can see the Stratosphere and the rest of the strip.

"Okay ..." I say.

I hear him run down the stairs onto the grassy knoll. Meanwhile, I walk through the apartment, through the kitchen and then stop to peer through the curtains down on him, but I can't get a good look because I don't have my contacts in. I'm wondering if he's my neighbor.

My neighbor is your typical Las Vegas shit head loser. I've not mentioned him because he's not worth mentioning. (Side note: let me just say: He is this guy who would stop by at queer hours and try to get me involved in his porno website with his wife. He had long blonde hair and was always spray-painting his electric guitar a new color. Maybe that's why I haven't mentioned him. I mean, the fact that we are both musicians and we both wound up in these apartments next to each other really just scared the shit out of me. Like this is the fate of musicians who don't make it or something.)

Anyway.

So I assume this "Colin" is really my porno website-neighbor. But I wasn't sure. So I go out on the balcony. And he starts yelling up at me, "Do you see that shit?"

I can barely see he's pointing at something.

"It's fucking UNREAL!"

I don't respond.

"Something *blew up*!" he says. "Over the city! It's a UFO! Or something! Look at that! Do you see it? OH MY GOD!"

I squint. I can't see anything.

"Er, no," I say. "I don't have my contacts in."

"*IT'S FUCKING REPTILIAN!*"

"Okay."

I stare out at the early dawn. Suddenly I can't take it anymore. "I gotta go put in my contacts!"

"Well you better go do it!" he says. "QUICK!"

"Okay!"

As I run to the bathroom, I'm thinking, what are the odds that a bomb has gone off at Nellis Air Force Base? It is just right outside of the city. Under 30 miles away. Or what if there was some other government explosion? Who knows what could have happened? They're doing missile tests out there all the time. They keep the ammo in underground bunkers. Do they still test fire nuclear missiles? And what's up with those chemtrails? (This would explain what happened with my heart!) Are these things legal? I often hear of radiation being a light residue in the Clark County water system.

I go into the bathroom. Flip on the light switch. But nothing comes on. Colin #1, my roommate, has apparently forgotten to pay the bill.

Goddammit Colin, I say.

I paid him this month! But apparently he didn't send in the money, because the lights aren't turning on. I put in my contacts. Make a moaning sound because they're not washed right.

"AHH!"

My eyes are burning.

I go back out on the balcony.

Nothing!

I look in the sky. There's nothing there. Apparently I missed the show. Well, that's not totally true. There is something. There is a star in the sky. And there's a funny looking bald guy out on the grassy knoll. And he's not wearing any shoes. And he's not wearing a shirt. He just has dirty jeans on.

"I'm sorry, I don't see anything," I say.

"WHAT?" he says. "You're kidding me! You're kidding me, right?"

"No."

"Look up at that star!"

"Is it Venus?"

"No!" he shouts. "That's no fucking STAR! That's an UPSIDE DOWN CROSS!"

I squint, trying to see what he's talking about. "Really? I'm sorry, I'm just not seeing it. But just out of curiosity, what drugs did you take last night?"

He put his hands on his hips.

"NONE, man. I'm just HIGH on LIFE, man."

He shakes his head. I had stretched the limits of his patience. "I don't have time for this. Where's Randy?"

"Randy?"

Okay, maybe he's not crazy. He came here looking for someone that's not me. He's on a mission. "There's no Randy here," I say. "And if I may say - you and I, just so you know - we don't know each other."

He smiles. There's a hint of playfulness in his tone.

"Oh I know that!" he says. "I'm not a *freak*. You and I have never met before."

"We haven't met before."

"But Randy," he says, "is in there with you. So thus: You and I appear to have a *dilemma,* because I want to get in and you won't let me."

Uh-oh.

"And I know that this is her apartment," he says, "because for one, that's her aquarium on the side of your stairwell."

I smile, uncomfortably. "Uh, no, that's actually mine."

It is actually my aquarium. I found it in the trash.

"And for two," he says, "those are her cigarettes up on your balcony."

I look down at the cigarette butts by my foot. My roommate smokes every night after work and then puts them into a toasted cookie can.

"That's interesting," I say. "But how do you know that there are cigarettes up here?"

"Because," he says, "I smoked one of them when I climbed up on your balcony to turn off your power."

I clench my jaws. The uncomfortable playfulness that I've felt has slowly begun to die and is now being replaced by a new emotion.

Fear.

"You turned off my power?"

"Yes."

"Why did you do that?"

"I had to. Electricity affects my body."

He stood up tall and arched his spine.

"I do not believe we have officially met," he says, extending a hand out in the air. "My name is Thoth and I'm an Egyptian God. I have superhuman powers and have spent the last five days running through the desert being chased by the Masons and helicopters. This is my only safe refuge. I've been stalking you for days. I need to talk to Randy."

"That's nice," I say, interrupting him. "Do you have a web site?"

"As a matter of fact I do. I'm at www.thothman.com ... That's T-h-o-t-h ..."

As he recited the web domain, I pretended to grab a sheet of paper but I wasn't really writing anything down on it because I was too busy *calling the police.*

"I'm going to go inside the apartment to write this down," I say. "I'll see you in second? Okay Thoth?" I smile, nod, and back up while locking the balcony door.

He's down there pointing, winking, and smiling.

I duck down so as not to be seen through the curtains. I race into my roommate's room and begin frantically calling 9-1-1.

"This is dispatch," the woman says on the other end of the line. "What is your emergency?"

"Crazy guy – outside my place – climbing up on my walls – won't go away."

"Have you taken any drugs this morning, Mr. Heffel ... Heffer ..."

"No, this is real."

"Well okay. Okaay." I hear buttons being pushed in the background. She was probably tracking my whereabouts. "Just hold tight. We'll send a car out there."

"Thank you."

I hang up the phone. Run through the living room. Look out the balcony door. He isn't there. But then I hear something at the front door. It sounds like he's knocking. I creep over and poke my eye through the peephole.

He's been listening to me to me this whole time talking to dispatch.

"I gotta get going Leo! Something came up!" he shouts. "Bye!" Then he tears down the stairwell, off into the concrete jungle.

I stand there in my underwear.

Later in the day, I called up Destiny. My voice was freshly infused with adrenaline. I told her the entire story. "… and then after he left I found that there was no more food out in the cat dish."

I told her I had been waiting in my home all day for the police, who never showed up. So I just was sitting there in the dark, munching on Chinese food, all alone.

"Well, Leo," she said, matter-of-factly, "I am sensing that you need to be very careful right now. Dark forces are all around you right now, and they are closing in."

"Dark forces? What?"

I didn't want to hear this type of lingo right now. I mean, I had to ask myself why had I not made it more clear to Destiny that …

"I'm not *that* spiritual."

"Excuse me?"

"That we need to be using terms like *dark forces*."

Long pause.

"It's just I'm not that religious," I said. "I'm bi. I believe in God and don't at the same time. I'm bi-gnostic."

I heard her tense up. Her breathing seemed to stop all together.

"Are you there?" I asked.

"*Oh my God*," she whispered. "Why have you not disclosed this part of yourself to me?"

"Well we've only been going out for four days and I feel like we've covered a lot of ground and I …"

"Oh no Bucko! *How could I be so stupid?* You are a PREDATOR. Telling me what I want to hear so that I'll sleep with you …"

"I … told you everything that I feel was …"

"FUCK FUCK FUCK! Well you know what? I don't feel that I can be with someone who is not as spiritual as I am!"

"I am as spiritual as you are! In fact, I'm MORE spiritual than you!"

"You just told me you're bignostic!"

"Yes and if you read Kierkegaard you will discover that the truly religious man makes a leap of faith only *after* doubt enters the mind.

And thus the layman can *teleologically suspend the ethical.* In Latin, telos means ..."

"Spare me the academia, professor - you know how much I hate Socrates. Do me a favor and return my book and sweater."

Click.

Chapter 30

ROMEO AND JULIET

4.6.07

Even with the stolid fact that I needed to escape hell (Vegas) and that if I worked things out with Destiny I would still be stuck in hell (Vegas) with the little beasts (8th graders) I could not help but answer her text message.

I'M LONELY, it read.

ME TOO, I typed back.

And there was nothing that I could do to avoid getting back in the "Let's Make a Baby" cycle again. You know. Well, after one of our intense cycles, lying in bed, staring up at the ceiling, Destiny had an epiphany.

"You know, Leo. I think that you really should be nice to him."

I almost couldn't fathom what she was saying. "Who? The stalker? You don't mean the stalker!"

"Well he didn't try to *harm* you. He's obviously not dangerous."

I thought about it.

"That's true," I said. "He only turned off the power because electricity bothers him. I wonder if Superman has the same problem."

But seriously, she did have a point. He didn't try to rape me.

4.11.07

So the next time the stalker came over, I decided I would be nice to him. It is important to love everyone. Not all homeless people are dangerous. They're just misguided.

Knock. Knock. Knock.

And this time it was the middle of the day.

I looked through the keyhole.

"Oh, hi Colin. No, Randy's not here. No, you can't come in."

His bald head bobbed up and down.

"But," I said, "why don't you go out on the front lawn? I'll go out on the balcony, and you'll be way down on the grass, and we can talk like we did last time?"

"Okay," he replied.

This could be fun. It was time to stop jamming on my piano keyboard, anyway. Five hours was about my limit.

Be nice to him, rang through my head.

I opened the drapes and looked down. There he was, down on the grass. *Was he masturbating?* No. I slid open the balcony window. Pulled my new red shirt over my head. I just bought it with my new teacher money. Eighty dollars. With the light shining in my hair, I must have been a really spectacular sight.

It was sunny out today.

"So Colin," I said. "Let's be frank here."

He nodded attentively.

"I don't want to be mean or anything," I said. "But I didn't really *buy* what you were saying the other night about the giant cross in the sky and the superhuman powers. Because superhuman powers don't exist. And then the part about the helicopters chasing you ..."

"There are helicopters," he said, interrupting me. "There are!" He stared up at me. "Would you just look at us!" he said, amused with the situation. "And I didn't believe you, like when you said that Randy doesn't live here, either."

We laughed together. I shook my head.

"She doesn't!" I said, giggling. "If that's the problem, if Randy is getting between our friend-ship or whatever this is we might have, let me go and get my mail. That way, we can look on the addresses wherein I can prove to you that she doesn't live here."

Why didn't I think of this before? I went back inside, ran into the kitchen area and grabbed some mail off the counter. Then I went back out and threw my junk mail down to him.

One by one, he picked the letters off the grass, and read them aloud. "Colin Spencer."

"That's my roommate," I said. "His name is Colin, too. How weird, huh?"

"Leo Heffel ... Heff ..."

"Heffelapfle. That one is me."

"Wow," he said, scratching his head. "Well this is the proof, I guess."

"Yeah," I said. "Man it's hot out here. Are you thirsty? Would you like a Diet Coke?"

"YEAH!"

I went back into the kitchen and grabbed a Coke. And then I got some Goldfish crackers. I strolled back out on the balcony and threw the Coke can down to him.

"Are you hungry?" I asked.

"I'm starving."

"Good."

He looked at me, wondering what I was up to.

"Now you can only have the Goldfish crackers," I said, "if you catch them in your mouth."

He looked up at me with an odd reaction.

"No using your hands," I said.

He thought this over before just agreeing to the rules.

"Yeah, I'm up for it," he said. "I'll do anything for food right now."

I threw a Goldfish cracker down to him. He hopped in the air like a dolphin. It hit his chin, and then went in the grass. When he reached down to grab it, I said, "No. You can't eat the ones that you don't catch. Or you don't get anymore."

He looked up at me, sourly.

"If you're good, I have candy, too."

A few days later I saw Destiny. I ran up to her and gave her a big hug.

"That nice thing really worked, thanks baby," I said, kissing her on the lips. I followed her inside her house and sat down at the table.

"See?" she said. "That's because you're an angel."

"Well, I know."

"No," she said. "I mean, a literal angel."

She stared at me.

I just stared back at her.

"*Oh my God Leo,* you don't know, do you?" she said. Her voice was filled with wonder and conviction.

I shook my head back and forth.

"*Even Cynthia knows,*" she said. (Her best friend.) (Worships her.)

"She does?" I asked.

I was about to argue with her, when I caught myself. *Remember what happened last time.* ("You are a PREDATOR! … You said that you are SPIRITUAL! … Give me my book back, Socrates.") So instead, I said, "Well, it would explain a lot."

She hugged me, and whispered, "My very own angel."

And then I fucked her.

4.12.07

I came home to my apartment the next morning, after a long night of "feeding the juniper plant" and bipsycholing. *So what if she thinks I'm a literal angel?* There could be worse things. At least she loves me.

I went up my stairs. Noticed the cat dish was empty. Huh. Went inside. Walked through the kitchen. *Is there a slight draft in here?* I turned the corner to watch some TV and ... *OKAY.*

Glass was scattered everywhere. The gigantic picture window, where it used to be, on the balcony, wasn't there anymore. *Holy shit.*

My heart began to pick up. I grabbed my cell phone. The maniac! *He could be in the apartment! He could still be in the apartment!*

"Hello this is dispatch."

"Hi 9-1-1, uh, this is Leo Heffelapfle again and I had a break in and I think I know who did it."

I could hear phone numbers ringing in the background and other operators talking all at once.

"Okay, we'll send a squad car over but it will be awhile."

"What?" This really unnerved me. "How come?"

"Well it is Mother's Day, sir."

"So?"

"This is the most violent day of the year."

"Oh. Okay."

"Just hold tight, sir."

"Okay."

After searching the rooms to see if "Colin" was still in the apartment, I began looking around to see if anything had been stolen. Five hundred dollars had been taken from the countertop. I was going to use that to fix my car. Normally I don't leave money around. And the one time I do, this happens. And someone ate half of my pizza. I turned over the Goldfish cracker carton. Empty.

I sat back down on the couch.

No shit, I waited in my apartment all day. I called the police at nine in the morning - they didn't show up until like 11:30 at night.

"Do you think you know who was responsible for the break in?" the cop asked. He was a big guy, jotting down everything I said onto a little yellow notepad.

"Yeah, I think I know who did it."

"What's his name?"

"I don't know. Colin something." I smiled nervously. "He's this guy who comes over and ... I get up on the balcony and he's down below on the grass."

His pencil stopped moving on the tablet.

"Romeo and Juliet."

He shut the tablet. "You better tell the other guys this story."

"Okay."

He called damn near half the force in and I'm surrounded by cops in my kitchen. "And then he says he's Thoth and that he turned off my power."

They laughed, grunting - even the women laughed like that. Like fucking pigs. And they all came in dragging their mucky, oily boots from out in the rain soaked night, completely destroying my carpet.

"That's quite a story," one of the investigators said. "Now you just need to rewrite the report on this college-ruled paper. It's your statement of what happened. Be very methodical. And can I give you a piece of advice?"

"Yeah, sure."

"To make sure we catch this psycho," he said, going through my cabinets, until he found a box of pretzels. "Word it 'I very strongly believe that Colin broke into my apartment.'" He dipped the pretzels into some dip from the fridge. "And then say – are you getting this?" He looked at me just holding the pen.

"Yes," I said, writing quickly.

"Say 'I very much believe that Colin was going to kill me.'"

"Okay," I said.

"And can I give you another piece of advice?"

"Yes sir."

"The next time you call us on Mother's Day, if you want our attention, say 'shots fired.'"

"Yes sir. Thank you sir."

I was in no mood to go to work the next day. I called in to the secretary to try and get out of it, but apparently the substitute teachers had heard about my room, and they refused to sub in there.

"I'm sorry, Leo, but we'll need you to come to school today."

"But I was up all night with my stalker."

I could tell she had me on speaker phone. I could hear the evil secretaries in the background laughing like witches.

"I'll be there in a minute," I said.

Chapter 31

SCARED SHITLESS

4.18.07

Now I must tell you that it was no fun to go and teach 8th graders only to go home at the end of the night and get stalked.

To go inside my house, fucking exhausted, and then to find the balcony door is unlocked. (???) *I just had the glass replaced.* How could Colin #1, my roommate, be so fuckin' stupid? Leave the balcony door unlocked? After what happened? Or what about me? Did I do it? Who did it? My anger was unquenchable. Like John McEnroe.

This is unacceptable, I muttered in my mind, going through the kitchen sink dish pile looking for a butcher knife. Peanut butter and jelly was all over it, making a fucking mess.

"You here?" I shouted.

I opened the closet. Looked under the bed. Opened the shower curtain. Nope. I examined the balcony door. Seems that the metal along the door latch was mangled, as if someone had been trying for a very long time to get in.

"This is *ridiculous*," I said. I was sick of it. Sick of 8th graders. Sick of living in fear. So I decided I was just going to buy a handgun at Walmart. Shoot him two times in the leg the next time he decided to pop in for a visit.

"There," I would say, standing above him like Clint Eastwood, "now don't you feel dumb?"

4.19.07

Before I actually made a purchase, I thought it might be a good idea to go and practice my shooting skills with Mr. Hartman, the Spanish teacher. He always had a small stockpile of paintball armor and guns in the back of his car. Over lunch he would sometimes show off his bruises and welts from the tournaments he went to over the weekends.

"Yeah sure I'll play with you," he said, as the fucking monsters ran past us in the hallway. "HEY, SLOW DOWN!" he yelled at them and then turned to me. "But you would never play with me before. Why are you suddenly interested now?"

"Let's just say I have a score to settle."

He just stared at me. "You doing okay?"

I stared at the 8th graders hitting each other in the distance. Fucking sociopaths. Narcissists. Throwing shit at me. Every day.

"Yeah I'm fine," I said.

I had spent the night before creating a fort in my bedroom made out of blankets and bookshelves and old mic stands. I set up a concrete block to hide behind, right outside my bedroom door. Practiced what it would be like shooting at him in slow motion, dodging behind the couch. Leg shot, kneecap blown off. Practice: strangulation maneuver. Practice: peanut butter and jelly butcher knife right in the butt.

4.20.07

The male teachers sat together at lunch, and the female teachers sat together - at separate tables. We felt that the female teachers were sexless, neurotic bitches, and they no doubt felt we were fat sexist pricks.

At least we talked about things like science. Dr. Cousteau had traveled the world in a blimp and undersea carriage studying marine wildlife. Mr. Schendel had spent all of his last paycheck on the blackjack tables. And I had a stalker.

"If this stalker enters your home, you must shoot him," Mr. Damon said. Geography teacher.

"NO!" said Dr. Cousteau. "If you do, you must shoot him in the head!"

I could feel the women from the other table notice our conversation for the first time in years.

"Because if he lives, then he can sue you," he continued.

"I don't give a fuck," Mr. Schendel said. "I sleep with a 9mm under my pillow. If some fucker came in my home, the rest of you would have to help me bury him."

"Now now," said Mr. Crux. He was the health teacher and had taught up in Browning, Montana for some time. "It is against the law to shoot someone unless they have a weapon."

"Plant it," said Mr. Hartman, "in his hand right before you shoot him, make him hold it."

"If you just shoot him," Dr. Cousteau said, "then you're going to go to jail for at least a year."

"Even if it's a head shot?" I asked.

"Oh yes."

Which was extremely disheartening. Could I tazer him? I needed to find a lawyer, and quick. I mean, was I just supposed to be a sitting duck? I was reminded of my 8th graders, and how all the power had gone to the students, and the teachers were at their mercy.

Chapter 32

THE END OF THE INNOCENCE

4.22.07

So meanwhile, Destiny had become obsessed with helping my music career. Her goal was to help artists achieve their dreams, of one I was which. But it made me a little apprehensive to get involved on a business level with the woman I was trying to procreate with, so I told her to take the music slow.

"Want to come over tonight?" she asked, swooning over the phone.

"I don't know, baby. It's a little late. Ten o'clock is late for a school teacher."

"But you said you would come over."

"I know. But I said that at four in the afternoon. It's 10 now."

I could tell she didn't like my response. "Besides, tomorrow is the first day of their quarterly exams, so I want to make a good impression on the kids," I said. "We could get together, but that would compromise their education."

Of course I was the only one who knew that we hadn't learned a damn thing all year in my class.

"Okay, I understand," she said. "And I do have things to get done."

"Right. We both have things to do. Let's get together tomorrow night."

"Sure. It's just that ..."

"Yes?"

"You promised we'd get together *tonight*."

"Well we can," I said, "but it's just that I'd have to get to sleep pretty early, that's all ... the kids' education."

She was quiet for a really long time, until she finally said, "Well I wanted to stay up and talk. That's the kind of mood I'm in."

"Well normally I'd be up for it. But I guess I just don't feel like getting in a fight tonight."

"Fight? What do you mean?" she asked, sincerely.

"Well I mean, I'm just not in the mood. I've been playing music for the last four hours and I'm highly caffeinated. I'm an idiot when I'm caffeinated."

It's true. Caffeine is a big no-no for me. Just ask any of my kids. ("Mister, you become a different person when you're on caffeine." "What do you mean?" I would ask, with my eye twitching along its socket.)

"Okay baby, so I'm not 100 percent in control of my emotions right now. And you know how you can get," I said, opening Pandora's Box.

"What do you mean?"

"Honestly, honey, I just feel like you can be conflict-oriented sometimes, and I just don't want that tonight."

And that's when the needle skipped off the record.

"EXCUSE ME?"

"Well I ..."

"EXCUUUSE ME? I'm *sorry* but you just INSULTED me just now. I DON'T THINK I CAN BE WITH SOMEONE WHO THINKS I HAVE AN ANGER MANAGEMENT PROBLEM."

"Then don't."

And then I just hung up on her.

Threw the phone on the counter. And you know what? I didn't feel that bad about it. Which was probably a good indicator that we weren't supposed to be together. I just didn't care.

And no kidding, like one second later, there was a knocking at the door.

I went over to it and looked through the peephole. Colin was there, crouched down, trying to listen in through the keyhole.

I went over and grabbed my phone. *This time I'm gonna get you, fucker.* I dialed 9-1-1.

"Hello this is dispatch," the lady said.

"Hi, I'm uh investigation number 44759-00134," I whispered into the line.

"Okay and where is the suspect now?"

I could hear Colin running down the stairs and then around the side of the house. "I don't know," I said. "Oh wait, there he is."

I could hear him, climbing up the side of the wall. "Uhhh," he said.

"He's, uh, climbing up my wall."

"Just hold tight, Mr. Heffelapfle, police will be there in a minute."

I could feel the adrenaline picking up in my body. I was just frozen. Do I stay in the hallway? Run into my fort? Get behind the concrete block? Run the drills like we practiced? I didn't even have a gun. I should've got a gun. I knew this was going to happen.

"Where is he now?" the dispatch lady asked.

And that's when I heard him land on the balcony. BOOM.

"Balcony."

I began to pant. "Huh-huh."

"Just relax Mr. Heffelapfle. Police will be there shortly."

He was shining a flashlight in through the curtains.

"Huh-huh. He's shining a flashlight in through the curtains. You know, like a burglar?"

"Just relax Mr. Heffelapfle."

BOOM.

"What was that sound?"

It was his foot, kicking with all its might, into the front of the balcony window, like he did last time.

"Shots fired shots fired!" I whisper.

BOOOOM!

I look at the door. Should I run? I grab my microphone stand — figured I'd use it like a baseball bat.

BOOOOOM!

"He's trying to kick in the window," I say, accelerating my speech. "*Shots fired! Shots fired!*"

"Don't worry, Mr ..."

And before she can give me any instructions, I just say the first thing that comes to my mind:

"STOP!"

The kicking stops.

"STOP!" I yell, "I'M IN HERE! DON'T COME IN!"

The air from the air conditioner kicks off.

The house is filled with silence.

And then.

And then I hear, "LEEEO? LEEO? Oh! Hi Leo, it's me, Colin!" His voice is rather cheerful. "Don't worry! I'm not dangerous! I'm just going to break in like I did last time!"

"WELL DON'T!" I scream. "I'M INSIDE!"

I look at my cell phone, and whisper, frantic-like, "Suspect is outside ... is outside my balcony window and has just *admitted* that it was he who broke into my place last time. Huh-huh."

"What's he saying now?" she asks.

I look at the window shade.

"But hey Leo!" he yells.

"Yes?" I say.

"You know what? I don't know if you're my FRIEND anymore!" His tone is becoming darker. "Wanna know why? Because you LIED to me!"

"What do you mean?"

Huh-uh goes my heart.

"You LIED to me!" he yells, clenching his teeth. "RANDY IS YOUR WIFE, AND YOU'VE GOT HER IN THERE, MOTHERFUCKER! YOU FUCKING PIECE OF SHIT!"

"Oh Jesus," I whisper into the phone. "He's pissed off. Suspect is pissed off!"

"FUCK IT FUCKER!" he shrieks. "I'm COMING IN!"

BOOM!

"Huh-huh. Huh. Huh."

"Mr. Heffel? Police are …"

BOOM!

"DON'T WORRY I'M NOT DANGEROUS! I'M JUST GOING TO BREAK IN AND STEAL 100 DOLLARS AND SOME FOOD BECAUSE I'M FUCKIN' STARVIN' MAN!"

"COLIN! WAIT!" I scream. And then … suddenly, I just … answer his plight. "Well why didn't you just *say* that, man?"

"Huh?" he says.

"I've *got* food in the refrigerator!"

He's silent. I can tell that my words are having an effect.

"If you get off my *balcony*, I'll *give* you some food!"

Again. There is a long moment of silence. My watch is ticking. Beads of sweat run down my face onto the floor. And then, he says the magic word.

"DEAL!"

The air conditioner kicks back on.

Holy shit! And then he leaps off the side of the balcony down onto the grass below.

"*Suspect…,*" I whisper into the phone, "*is off balcony.*"

"Okay," says the woman on the other end of the line, "now all you need to do is keep him there until the police arrive shortly. Stall him."

"*Okay,*" I whisper back.

Although I don't see him, I can imagine him outside on the front lawn, pacing.

"LEO!" he yells. "What are you doing?"

I open up the refrigerator. Look around. "JUST MAKING YOU A SAND-WICH! WHITE OR WHEAT?"

"WHITE!"

"LETTUCE? MAYO?"

"HOLD THE MAYO!"

"WOULD YOU LIKE A SIDE OF POTATOES WITH YOUR ORDER?"

I walk over to the window and look down through the curtain. The sandwich is in my hand. I can see him down below. He's looking up at me, distraught and hungry ... as suddenly ... suddenly, the ENTIRE area around him LIGHTS UP in a piercing, agonizing white light.

I look up in the sky.

"OH MY GOD!" Colin screams.

A giant helicopter descends right above my roof. WHOO-WHOO-WHOO go its blades blowing and its throwing of dust – everything, everywhere.

Colin looks up at the helicopter, and then looks up at me.

I bite into his sandwich.

At seeing this, he flips me off. (Both hands, because two middle fingers are better than one.)

And that's when this absolute beast, this giant seven-foot monster cop springs out of the bushes, I mean right out of nowhere, running at Colin like a diesel truck, yelling:

"STOP MOTHERFUCKER! STOP MOTHERFUCKER! STOP MOTHER FUCKER!"

When Colin sees this, his whole body shakes and turns into liquid Jello. I mean, he almost faints right there as his legs fail to move like a derby car spinning its wheels, burning rubber. And then, well, either all that adrenaline kicked in at the same time or he must actually have superhuman powers, because he ran and then jumped over the side of the fence – I mean he *launched* over it like a fucking Olympic vaulter.

And then the monster cop did, too, running after him, down the side of the street.

Cop car after cop car whiz by and then another helicopter, flashing its spotlight.

I looked back at the phone that was lying there on the counter.

I went over to it. Picked it up.

Dial: Destiny.

"Hello?" she said.

"Hey baby, it's me," I said, whispering. "Can I come over?"

There was no answer.

"Listen, I …" I began. "I've had a change of heart."

There was still no answer.

"And that stuff about the dark forces? You're right - I think. And I'm an angel. A literal angel."

Still no answer.

"I love you."

And then.

"LISTEN BUCKO. I'M NOT THE ONE WHO HAS THE 'ANGER MANAGEMENT PROBLEM.' DO YOU UNDERSTAND ME? DO YOU UNDERSTAND ME, YOU SON-OF-A-BITCH! YOU FUCKING COCKSUCKER! **YOU** HAVE THE …"

But before I could answer, the phone hung up. I had run out of minutes. Or didn't pay my bill or something. So she thought I hung up on her, but didn't.

This would be our last interaction.

Not that I cared.

Fifteen minutes later, there was a knocking at the door. The police were there, and they had caught Colin. They asked me to go outside and identify him.

"Okay," I said.

When I went out to the parking lot, I saw him sitting in the back of a cop car. And when he saw me, he smiled. And it's hard to describe what the smile looked like, other than to say it was cute, like a little boy. Because this was the game we played. This was our world.

I motioned to the policeman to unroll the window.

When he did, I gave Colin his sandwich.

PART III

Chapter 33

MR. FIEHR'S SPEECH

5.2.07

When I went back to school, I was so drained, that I just *had* it. The kids, the shitty spring break, the stalker, Destiny leaving me, the librarian, with her yelling at me, and everyone else going crazy – my fucking life sucked.

And thus fifth period was walking all over me, too. No one would be quiet. No one would let me speak.

"Five-four-three-two-one. QUIET."

They kept on talking.

"Mariana, up against the wall."

"What?" she shot back. "No. Why? Why? Why? Why?"

Ah, the Ricardo defense pattern. But much like a bacteria building up new resistances, I was the antibiotic that no longer worked.

"I'm not arguing. Go. Now!"

"Why? Why? Why?"

"Okay, bye. I'm kicking you out to Hartman's."

"NOOO!" she shouted. (She and Hartman seriously did not get along. Apparently they had been enemies in past lives. "*She haunts me in my dreams,*" he would tell me over lunch.) "Okay, I'll be good."

"Five-four-three-two-one!" I yelled at the class.

They all kept talking, which started Mariana up again.

"Okay, bye Mariana."

It takes *time* to write up a slip to kick her out. *And* the rest of the students, one by one. Should I start screaming and yelling and throwing books down? It appears to be the only way. No. Keep kicking kids out. One at a time. But soon there'll be no class left and then Patricia will probably come to advise me as I'm standing giving a great lecture to no one. I can try calling parents who are never there. *That* will take all period, using up *my* phone minutes.

So I just said, "Okay guys, since you won't be quiet and insist on being jerks, here's the worksheet. Raise your hand if you need help because I'm not talking over this noise."

This girl named Georgia said, "He doesn't know how to teach."

For some reason, this really rattled me. "I'm sorry, Georgia. *I didn't quite catch that.*"

"I didn't say anything."

"She didn't," another helper organism said. Ping. Ping. They were getting more and more out of control. I looked at my floor. A fucking trash heap. I pictured myself on my hands and knees after school.

No. I'm not cleaning up their shitcan.

"And they get away with it as usual," I heard the librarian echo through my mind. "Old Mr. H. is the fool, pulled another one over *his* eyes ..."

No.

I'm going to nuke these fuckers.

I got up and decided to go next door. End their little "party" by going to get Anne Marie the rapist.

Oh! And look who's here! Even better!

Mr. Fiehr.

"Excuse me," I said. "Mr. Fiehr, would you mind helping me, get the students to clean my floor?"

He nodded. Mrs. Fiehr came with him. "This is the SAME class that spit on his chairs," she said.

"And stole the candy you bought me," I said.

I could see the fury lighting up in his eyes. His pony tail danced across his shoulders like an angry mongoose.

We busted down my door.

"EVERYONE! PICK UP THE TRASH *NOW!*" Anne Marie yelled.

"You think you're a funny guy?" her husband said, getting in the face of Eddie.

"THERE'S DIRT IN THESE CORNERS! MOVE IT!" Anne Marie yelled.

The kids got up and roamed about the room like piranhas eating the flesh off mega fauna.

"NOW! Put your heads on your desks! You too, Eddie!" the Fiehrs screamed in unison.

All the kids did as they were commanded to by their mothers before their fathers came home to beat the shit out of them.

Mr. Fiehr began to wander about the room. "You all come to this class and make A-S-S-E-S out of yourself everyday!" he screamed. "Well, it's going to stop now! We're here to HELP you! And in high school they're not going to put up with it! They're not going to put up with it, in LIFE! You ever heard of biting the hand that feeds you? WELL THAT'S WHAT YOU'RE DOING!"

He walked in between the rows. I could see Eddie and Angela trying not to laugh.

"You see the busboy behind JB's Big Boy digging through the trash? Do you think that he *meant* to work there? No, he was an 8th grader, just like you, not a care in the world, no *plan*. Well let me tell you, he didn't plan to be dumpster diving! On drugs! It all starts *here*, folks!"

"In my class," I said.

"This is where life begins. Welcome to life. You are born, now."

After class I went down to the office and handed in my resignation. I stated in my letter that I would at least finish out the rest of the year.

Chapter 34

THE COFFIN

5.3.07

The next day, I was in class trying to teach for the first time ever, when Captain America barged in. He was sweating, feverishly so.

"Go," he said.

"What?"

"Dr. North wants to see you in his office. I'll take over from here."

I clutched my heart. *I've never been inside his office.*

"Okay," I said, looking at my kids, who were all staring back at me. I couldn't help but to feel a little nervous. *Not that it matters.* I already handed in my resignation. It's not like I'm going to live in Vegas for the rest of my life.

Bamby was at her desk talking to North. Seemed like they were having a friendly conversation. When he spotted me, he smiled, but in that deceptive way that indicates that there is something deeper lurking underneath the waters.

"Come on in," he said, smiling that Joker grin. He had polished it well, for administrators. Smile. Then don't smile. Smile. Then don't smile.

We went inside his office.

He sat down behind his desk. There were numerous tiny helicopters on it - some were plastic and ticked with tiny clocks in them. Others were clear and glass.

"Well," he said, "the reason, (he flipped through a paper on his desk and actually appeared to be looking up my name), Leo, I am here talking with you today, and not Patricia, is because she is out this week, sailing in the Virgin Islands."

Behind him, on the wall, was a poster of a giant Apache helicopter. The missiles and rockets actually appeared to be aiming right at you as you sat in the chair in front of him.

"You know, while I was being trained in Desert Storm," he said, "there was this one Lieutenant who didn't like me very much. He even told me, to my face. He said that he was an A-type personality, and I, well, wasn't. After a raid in which we would kill Iraqi forces, he liked to go home in silence. I didn't. I liked to have barbecues and throw parties. This, for some reason, bothered him. Patricia," he said, taking a deep breath, "is like that Lieutenant. She doesn't like you, for the reasons she has. And me, I'm caught in the middle. There are administrators over here, teachers over there, parents over there, putting on the squeeze," he said. "But one thing that Lieutenant said to me, years later, after the war was done, was that even though we had different styles, I certainly got the job done. And it was scary. It was *scary* going in there, for the first time, when I had only been trained on video games to now be out there actually in the real field, much like you and those kids, I am sure. But, unlike my Lieutenant who told me I got the job done, your Lieutenant feels that you didn't."

I sat there, scratching my chin.

"See, you have to realize, that the Apache helicopters that we trained you to fly, you were flying too fast, and too low to the ground. You became a *danger* to your own crew mates. A danger to your own self. And that's why we had to pull you out of there, out of the classroom, before you hurt someone. And that's why Patricia decided, in conjunction with the School Board, to take this action, to Court Marshall you."

"What?" I said.

"Open the door," he said.

A Priest and a Chaplain came into the room from behind me, wafting incense and bells. BONG. BONG.

They stood on either side of Dr. North, in front of the Apache helicopter.

"I'm not going to sugarcoat it," he said, serving me my non-renewal papers. "May you rest in peace."

"Wait ..." I tried to say.

"Never again, Leo HEFFELAPFLE," he shouted, holding the papers in the air, "SHALL YOU SERVE HERE, YOU SPINSTER! YOU SERPENT OF EVIL, GODLESS WHORE, IN CLARK COUNTY AS A TEACHER. MAY YOUR SOUL BE MARKED AS IMPURE MAY YOUR FIDELITOUS RELATIONS REMAIN CELIBATE! MAY YOU GO BACK TO THE PLACE YOU CAME, DRAGON, DOWN INTO THE MUCK AND MIRE, FILTH AND ROT, AND IF YOU EVER TAKE IT UPON YOURSELF TO HIDE THIS PERIOD IN YOUR LIFE,THEN, WELL, YOU'LL GO TO JAIL."

"I don't understand," I interrupted. "I already resigned. I'm not coming back. Why is this even necessary?"

"Because that's how Patricia wants it."

I suddenly became cross. "What?"

"You know, Leo, one day I destroyed 57 Iraqi tanks ...," he said. "It was a really big day. They were weak, and I was strong."

The Priest put a piece of bread on my tongue.

"But I was trained how to fly Apache Helicopters, and they weren't," he said.

"I was never trained," I said. "I never had a mentor. Not a real one."

"Right, and that's a 50 million dollar piece of machinery you're flying, boy. Each one of them, each little 8ᵗʰ grader has their own mold, just like you, and you can't change who you are. You were destined for something else." He motioned toward the priests. "Roll in the casket."

"What?" I said, haphazard and jumpy.

"I don't like this, either," he said. "I like barbecues."

"I don't understand," I said.

"You listened to your parents, now look what happens," he said, as the tall shirtless executioner came from behind me, and put the plastic bag over my head.

"At one point, you've got to start thinking for yourself," he said, tears welling up in his eyes. "But by the time you figure that out, it's often too late."

After much struggling, I began to lose consciousness. The last words that I heard my principal mutter were to the chaplain. "Goodbye my son."

At some point I woke up. I was in the coffin. It was dark.

"I'm dead," I said. "Life is over."

But then.

I don't know what came over me, but I heard something faint and distant. A small voice. And I listened to it. *Get up.* What? *Get up.*

What had become of me?

I opened up the heavy wooden lid. *Daylight.* Apparently they just placed the coffin in front of the school. Didn't have enough in their budget to bury me alive.

I straightened out my clothes, got up, and went back inside.

Chapter 35

THE FIRE EXTINGUISHER

5.20.07

Today there was an evil that pulsed through the halls of Water's Gate middle school.

It all started in third period with Poison Ivy, Slutty-Portia, and Scorpio Loins Jezebel engaging me in a three-pronged attack. While Jezebel talked to me about why her grades were so low, Poison Ivy crawled on her hands and knees up to my desk. Once there, she began searching the cupboards until she found my shaving cream. (It's the good kind, perfect for rough beards.)

Thus, while Portia tried to give head to Lancelot in the hallway, Poison Ivy attended to higher things, namely, shooting shaving cream all over my computer.

This of course enraged me.

Poison Ivy passed the shaving lotion off to her best friend and scapegoat, Jezebel, who by the way is slightly less advanced than is usual for one's age, so that the full weight of my rage would be known to all.

When the bell rang, on their way out the door, the students pulled the fire extinguisher, filling the room with smoke.

"STOP!" I yelled at Lancelot and Portia. But they escaped.

I went down to the Dean's office.

"Did you catch who did it, Mr. Heffelapfle?"

"No, but I think it was Lancelot. He was right next to the device at the time of the gassing."

"Okay. So you didn't see who did it precisely?"

"No."

"Then you want me to ...?"

"So I should just let it go?"

"Yes."

Period four. More evil girls. Witches really. Maria, my secret crush, Lacey the ho-bag and Obloquy Ramona arrived half an hour late to class, as usual. The fire extinguisher smoke was a perfect entrance for the witches, who started coughing and faking asthma attacks as soon as they entered the room. (Falling on the ground, holding their throats.)

When Lacey and Maria discovered that their report cards were less than divine, (surprisingly they were both flunking), Lacey went on a verbal rampage.

"On the count of five, class, yell Mr. Heffelapfle is a faggot!" Lacey shouted.

"Lacey, stop," I said.

"1-2-3-4-5!"

"MR. HEFFELAPFLE IS A FAGGOT!" shouted the class.

"Guys, knock it off," I said to the room. "Lacey, you're going to the Dean's."

"No I'm not. It wasn't me. It was the whole class, wasn't it guys. 1-2-3-4-5!"

"MR. HEFFELAPFLE IS A FAGGOT!"

"See?" Lacey said. "It's *them*."

"You're obstructing peace," I said, writing down a Dean's referral. "Causing a riot."

Then, the air seal on the fire extinguisher had apparently burst because its hose began spraying in the air like one of those yard toys that kids run through on hot summer days. I ran over to it to try and turn it off but the hose part squiggled and then wrapped its muscular plastic around my body like a giant python.

I fell to the ground, wrestling it, but losing.

Slowly losing air. Must breathe.

At this, of course, the kids screamed, terrified, and went running out of the room.

"STOP! STOP!" I shouted.

"FAGGOT!" Lacey yelled, running out of the room. I threw the extinguisher into the closet, breaking everything inside. I beeped the buzzer. No one. "*Help* ..." I said into the white button on the wall as my room completely filled with smoke.

I went outside, only to see my students running away. Not all of them. A few of them were still there.

"Get back here, Lacey! Get back here, Maria!" I shouted. These were the only two I really cared about retrieving because they were going to pay for their little "comments."

The class and I stood outside for about five minutes in silence.

"The room is fine," I said, putting a chair in the door. "Just gotta let it air out a little."

"I'm not going back in there," Maria said. "It's a health hazard."

"Yeah," agreed Willy, "I'm going to stay outside and soak up the rays."

"No you're not." I opened the door of promise to my room. "It's already aired out, guys. Look. Smell that. Ah. Fresh air in my class. Come back inside."

One by one, I reiterated the importance of getting back in. They wouldn't go through and I was forced to lose it. "GET INSIDE! NOW!"

"Geez, you don't have to yell, mister. We were going to do it," Willy said.

Everyone entered - back into the smoke-filled room.

"Now you have the worksheet on homonyms," I said. "Fill it out. It's easy. Too sounds like to sounds like toe sounds like tow. What's it going to be? Fill in the blank."

I sat down at my desk, not believing that this was my job. I looked up to see Ramona coming at me.

"Mister," she whispered.

"Yes?"

"*Why do you let them treat you like that?*"

"Like what?"

She pointed at the class. "*Them. All of them. They walk all over you.* It's really DISGRACEFUL. I can't believe my eyes."

I looked at my clothes. I was covered in fire extinguisher dust. I held up a mirror. My face was all white. There was shaving cream all over my computer. I looked at my students, suddenly very, very upset.

"You make me SICK!" I yelled at them.

Ramona sat down.

"Uhhh, I'm not feeling good, mister," Maria yelled.

I looked over and saw some of the other kids who were pretending to cough from the smoke, too.

"Oh no, I'm not the one who is 'sick' here - it is YOU!" I shouted at her. "You make ME sick!"

"No, I really am," she said

"Yes she is," Lacey said. "She's turning *green*."

"You're not sick," I said. "You know what that's called?" I grabbed a magic marker and began to spell on the board. "That's called hy-po-chon-dria. Can anybody here tell me what this means?"

At this, Maria fainted and fell unconscious on the floor.

"MARIA!" Lacey screamed.

"Shut up, stop joking. Not funny, Maria," I said.

I walked over to her.

Wait a minute.

"Maria," I said, slapping her face. "Wake up." She was turning green. I ran over to the button on the wall. "HELP!"

No answer.

And then began the sprint. I should have sent a student for help, *but they would fuck it all up*, I was thinking, and *the Dean's is only a good 30-yard sprint away.* Which I did, running past Mrs. Pee's kids who were jogging around the track at the same time.

"GET OUT OF MY WAY!" I screamed, plowing through them like bowling pins.

One kid actually sped up and tried to beat me, but at the last moment I pushed him into the wall.

I ran inside the Dean's office.

"GIRL FAINTED! MY ROOM! MR. HEFFELAPFLE'S! CALL AMBULANCE!"

The secretary just stared at me, and took another drink from her cup of coffee.

I reversed directions and sped back to my room. When I kicked open the door I hit Edgar in the face and he went flying onto the ground.

"She's not moving Mister!" I heard someone say.

"Where is she?" I asked, pushing through the mob of kids. It was so smoky that I could hardly make out where I was. When I saw her, I jumped on top of her, and began to administer mouth-to-mouth resuscitation.

"WE'RE GOING TO HAVE TO TAKE OFF THIS SHIRT!" I yelled. "OR AT LEAST WET IT DOWN! HERE, JESTER, WHATEVER YOUR NAME IS - GO AND FILL UP THIS WATER DOWN IN THE BATHROOM."

Is it five heartbeats and then breathe 15 or is it 15 hearts and then two mouths? I couldn't remember what I learned in CPR but no matter, the key is getting oxygen to her deprived brain.

My face moved in slow motion down toward hers, and the moment our lips touched, she awakened. Her eyes opened wide and, in seeing the situation, it must have proved to be too much of a shock to the senses, for she quickly fainted again.

Of course, need I mention that while this was occurring, somebody was spraying shaving cream all over my computer. The fire alarm had gone off so that the water sprinklers coated our young, lithe bodies with a fine sweat-like mist.

I guess I didn't notice that Patricia came in to make another observation of me, as Maria and I locked lips, once more.

5.21.07

"You should have taken those kids out," Mr. Irish said, over lunch. "Fire extinguishers have a chemical that sucks oxygen out of fires, and believe me, you don't want that in your lungs."

"Was it powder CO_2?" Dr. Cousteau asked me, chewing on a chicken ball.

"I don't know," I said.

"He doesn't know," said Mr. Irish, to Dr. Cousteau.

"Well you should have gotten them out of there," said the Doctor.

"You don't think I should have left them in there? The smoke was pretty much gone," I said.

"Why take the risk?"

I suddenly thought of Ramona. *Mister, they're walking all over you.*

And then in slow motion one-two-three-four-five. *Mr. Heffelapfle is a faggot a fucking faggot ... Mrrr. Heffffeeelllaaaapppfflle is a faaaaagootttt.*

Chub-by bun-ny.

I snapped back to reality.

"Fuck'em," I said. "Let'em hang. I hope they all die."

This caught the attention of all the teachers at the table. They exchanged private glances. The rest of the meal was silent.

Chapter 36
THE SUSPENSION PAPERS

6.6.07

"I had another dream that you murdered us," Cassandra said.

I was sitting next to her desk, with my feet outstretched, correcting papers. I gently laughed at her diagnosis of the future.

"Oh? Do tell."

"Yes," she continued, "and in it you told the class to stop making fun of you, and that you have friends now."

"Who were my friends?"

"You pulled out a sword and chainsaw."

"Well," I smiled. "Don't worry, that would never happen to me."

Mrs. Lansbury came knocking at my door. "Excuse me, sir, but Dr. North wants to speak with you."

"Okay."

When I went into his office, he was behind his desk. Sitting to the left of me, in her black dress, was Patricia with her yellow notepad and red pen ready to start writing. They both smiled. Wide.

"Good to see you Mr. Heffelapfle," he said. "We're here to serve you your papers for the days you are to be suspended, seeing as killing you doesn't seem to work."

The three of us laughed and I clapped my hands together.

"Can't kill me," I said.

"But I just want you to know," he said, becoming more solemn, "that when you come back to work, after the two weeks, if I hear of any *disruptions* coming from your class, then I will be forced to physically remove you from the classroom."

Again, I looked up and saw the looming poster of the Apache helicopter staring down at me. I imagined him using force on hundreds of Iraqis.

"Okay," I said.

"Teachers talk," he said. "Word gets around. Don't think that I don't know what happened with the fire extinguisher."

"Yeah. Well," I said, "I'm not taking responsibility for that."

"As a teacher, it is your responsibility."

"No, as a principal, it is your responsibility."

Patricia subtly rubbed her legs together. Golden sparks danced between them. This caught both of our attentions, and I realized that we were now about to lock horns for a trophy of some kind. Or at least he was.

And I didn't want any part of this. So I backed down. "It's no use arguing over this."

"But it is your responsibility," he said.

"Don't make me match you point for point. Just let it be known that I passionately disagree, and that by law the Nevada State Firefighters' Association put extinguishers in teachers' rooms and if I touch them then I go to jail."

"You should have removed it," he said.

"What?"

"You should have torn it off the wall."

"It's not my responsibility."

"Yes it is."

"*You're* the ones who put *me* the *new teacher* in that room. I'm a *new* teacher. And *you* are in charge of the facilities. What - am I supposed to keep my eyes on the fire extinguisher eight hours a day as I'm teaching class?"

"You should have thought of it," he said. "In battle, Leo, anything can happen."

We locked eyes.

"But we're not in battle," I said.

That's when Patricia pushed her legs back together and said, "Excuse me, boys, but I'm going to go and make a copy of these suspension forms."

"Sure," we both said.

As soon as the door closed, the two of us began whispering.

"*I have to go with what she said*," he began. "*I'm in a tight spot, can't you see? Between you and her, it's nothing personal.*"

"*I know*," I whispered back. "But *you* don't see what *I* see. She acts *completely* different to you than she does to me and the rest of the 8th-grade teachers."

Patricia came back in. "The copier is not in use."

"Okay," we both said, straightening our backs.

Dr. North's fake smile came back on. "Well, Patricia and I have to get going. The bottom line, Leo, is that if I hear your name come up once over my walkie talkie, then that is it. You are out of here."

"Is this another one of your *hints*?" I asked.

He grimly nodded. "Yes it is." He pointed to my file on his desk. "Remember when last time I told you that you ought to leave, but you listened to your father?"

"Yes."

"And now look at where you are."

"So what are you saying?"

"We told those Iraqis to not go near the oil well. Problem was, they didn't understand English. You do understand English, and I'm hinting to you just like I did to the Iraqis." Suddenly his eyes began to water. "I'm also saying that in many ways, I am your father."

"And Patricia is your wife?"

"Yes," he said. "But I have to do what she says."

"What if that means killing your own son?"

Patricia looked at both of us, not sure of what to say.

"That would be God telling me to do that," he said, "through the woman."

Before I could ask him if he was going to tie up my limbs and drag me up Mount Moira, I suddenly recalled how earlier in the day, the Dean, Betty, kept sending me free referral slips.

I wonder what that was all about.

Teachers are given referral slips for bad students. But a bad student can't be referred until a number of lengthy and time consuming tasks are completed.

In other words, before a student is to be sent to the Dean's office, said teacher is supposed to have: 1. Had a student conference, 2. Called the parent, 3. Had a parent teacher conference, 4. Had a counselor conference, 5. Had an administrator conference, 6. Sent letters to all the other teachers inviting them to a conference, and 7. Planned an intervention with cake and lemonade.

ONLY THEN can said teacher send out the bad student from class.

Why? Because there is only one Dean for 2,000 students who are all on behavioral programs! And they hate me because I kick out the bad students rather than letting them pee on my floor!

Thus, why *would* the Dean, Betty, approach me in the hallway?

"Leo I can see you're going to need these Dean's referral forms," she had said, handing me 20 of them.

"But aren't you overloaded?" I asked. "I thought you *hated* me to send kids to you?"

"No, I don't mind," she said, smiling.

I wiped the sweat off my forehead. Betty and all the administrators, i.e., Patricia and North, were good friends. It would be relatively easy to make a teacher look bad, if that's what they wanted to do. And here Betty was, strangely telling me to skip all the little steps, which would only make me look like a moron on paper as they continued to build their case.

I was being framed. Somebody had to be the scapegoat to explain why the No Child Left Behind test scores in our building were so low, on average. And it had nothing to do with me forgetting to say "stop" on number 57 rather than number 58.

I looked at Patricia and her hand puppet, Dr. North. I could just imagine their conversation after I left the office:

"Mr. Heffelapfle thinks that we're close," Dr. North would tell her. "That he and I have a *private* friendship. He tells me everything."

"What did he tell you when I wasn't here?" Patricia would ask, her eyes lighting up like a hyena in one of those National Geographic videos.

"He told me that you treat me differently than the other teachers."

"Well isn't that the truth," she would say, unbuttoning her blouse.

I snapped back to the meeting.

"So you've got to contain those kids," Dr. North said, "during the last two weeks, when they are the craziest. They are going to be off the wall, and if they come at you or yell profanities or throw anything or do anything, you've got to keep them in the classroom, or else lose three months of summer pay."

"Okay."

"The choice is up to you," he said. "And hand in your lesson plans for the days you are gone."

"What?" I said. "Why should I have to hand in lesson plans if I'm not getting paid?"

"Because, Leo, you are still the teacher."

"If I'm not there I'm not the teacher."

"And whose fault is it that you got the suspension? It's yours."

"That's actually contentious."

I could see Patricia trying to hold back her evil black mamba smile. She was finally going to get the opportunity to kill Ricki Ticki Taffy. This was all power shit. JC was right. *She* was the one at the helm of this. *She* was piloting this helicopter. *She* was Karl Rove.

"Everyone's on my side," he said. "The superintendent, Patricia, and the Union have created a nice triangle assault formation. We've got all the cards, and you have got nothing."

"So just stay at home and relax Mr. Heffelapfle," Patricia said, "and watch TV."

"Yes. Stay at home," Dr. North said, "and come up with another gameplan. Some people just weren't meant to teach. You either got it or you don't and you don't. Are we all done here? Oh, and once you have those lesson plans all typed up, give them to Patricia, and if you decide to resign early," he said, winking at me, "then come and see me."

Chapter 37

THE TRUTH AT LAST

After the meeting, I went down to Anne Marie's room.

"Apparently they're going to use physical force to remove me from my class," I said.

"Huh? What? How do you know this?" she cried.

"Because I asked Dr. North if he was hinting when he said that he would remove me from the class and he said yes, just like he *hinted* to the Iraqis."

She shook her head. "Those bastards. Listen Leo, here's what you have to do. If I were you, I would stop grading all together. Just tell the kids to have a book open in front of them, and *pretend*."

"To pretend to be learning?"

"Yes."

"Should I give fake lessons?"

"Yes."

"With fake pencils and fake pieces of paper?"

"Yes. Fake it all. Tell the kids that they'll all get A's. That's what we do."

"What?"

"We *all* do it."

"Huh?"

She took a deep breath. "Now I wasn't going to tell you this, Leo, but I'm going to take a serious risk right now, because I think that you deserve to know. I just can't stand to see you in any more pain."

"What?" I asked. "Let me in on what?"

"The club," she said.

The closets in Anne Marie's room suddenly began to open, and all the teachers came out from inside of them, one by one. Mr. Hartman, Mr. Irish, Mrs. Krushney, Mr. Cousteau, oh and look, there's Mr. Schendel. Some were dressed in camouflage, and others carried machine guns and hand grenades.

"What the ..." I said.

"Yes," she said. "You somehow knew all along, didn't you."

"Well I had ideas but I ..."

"See," Mr. Ryder said. "I tried to tell you earlier. I was this close," he said, holding up his two fingers. "But if you couldn't accept the operation, then you would wind up blowing it for the entire Rebellion."

"Rebellion?"

"Yes, the Rebellion."

And at this, a dark figure walked out from behind the shadows.

Chapter 38

COCONUTS

So this teacher who has always kind of been in the back of my peripheral vision, who I had only one memorable conversation with, whose classroom was on the other side of the building, making him always just right out of reach, approached me from behind the shadows.

"Mr. Heffelapfle."

I smiled.

"Remember me? Mr. Morales." We shook hands.

"Yes, the teacher of the year," I said.

He stood in front of me, like some great tower. "I hear that you are still having some ... difficulties ... with the administration."

"Yes, I have."

His face turned red. "Now I wasn't going to tell you this, when you first got here, because you were too young, and I didn't know if I could trust you – but so have I – been having some problems. Dealing with that principal. He is doing things wrong, quite wrong." He lowered his voice as Mrs. Pee, Patricia's pet, went walking by.

"Get down! Get down!" Mr. Ryder said, pushing Mr. Hartman up against the wall.

And then Carol, Patricia's secretary, poked her head around the corner. But I didn't think she was spying for Patricia. I had a peculiar hypothesis that stated that Patricia was a mean bitch to everyone, and thus Carol spied on account of her own need for salvation, not on a need to see me endure more punitive measures.

When she left, Mr. Ryder released his grip and then patted Mr. Hartman on the shoulders. Mr. Morales continued.

"You need to help me nail this son-of-a-bitch," he said. "Have you pressed the Union against him?"

"Mr. North? No."

"Why not?"

I could tell that this angered him.

"Because I am afraid," I said, "if I piss him off, he'll screw me out of my summer pay. That's six thousand dollars."

"*Well you need to.*"

"I'm just trying to get through this fucker. Just get out of here. *Where's my money.* Boom. Gone."

He cracked his knuckles. But I could tell he understood.

"This principal," he said, "is what we Latinos refer to as a COCONUT."

"A coconut?"

"Yes. That's someone who appears Latino, who has the dark skin color, but is really a white person underneath."

"You mean … he has none of the culture?"

"Precisely! And so the district does this – hires people who look Latino because of the high ratio of Latinos in the schools, because it looks good, while not thinking it entirely through! Half of my kids don't even speak English."

"Same here," I said, my eyes watering. "I have one kid who can't even speak a word of English. I go and tell Patricia, and what does she do, but says to keep him in the room. And then he gets bored because he can't read anything so he has no other choice but to cause trouble."

There was a long pause. He looked at me with a stare that seemed to be asking if I believed that the situation was too far out of control. If I was too burnt out. If I had already lost hope.

Then the bell rang.

"I have kids waiting for me at the door," I said. "I have to go."

"No you don't, Mr. Heffelapfle. I've got your back," JC said, limping in from the hallway, with her cane.

"JC!"

"Yes," she said. "You just stay here, newbie. Here, I brought you some pizza."

"North came from Texas," Morales said. His voice was raspy and tough. "An old military buddy of his is on the School Board. They are tight. That guy got him the job. And they're cruel bastards, man. They might look nice and smile like you're their best friend, but that is not the case."

"That's the impression he gave to me." I ripped a slice off my warm pizza.

"Can I have a bite?" he asked.

"Yes, please go ahead."

He took an extra big bite.

"So let me tell you how it all started, Leo."

Chapter 39

JOIN US

"Last semester, when the leaves were still green," Morales said, "I had a young boy in my room named David who would not stop starting fights with the other kids. So I tell the Dean, Betty, to get him out of my classroom. Betty says she's 'too busy.'"

"I had the same types of problems," I said.

"So I go to the football coach, because this boy is on the team, and I tell him, 'Do NOT let this boy play in the next two games. His grades are low and he will not stop acting up in my class.' The coach looks at me like I am crazy. I say 'You know the rules.' The coach then goes to the Dean. And I think progress has been made because they pull the kid out of the next two games. But then I find out through some kids that the Dean said to David: 'Oh you are having trouble with this teacher? Well what you need to do is get some of your friends together who share the same story and then come back to me.'"

"Right."

He sipped his coffee. "And so then when I get wind of this I go right up to North in the hallway and say 'You're not running this place right.' Now, side note. While North may be a coconut, he still believes on some level that he and I are alike." He crinkled his eyebrows. "That is his biggest error.

"Now, in the moment, it's true that I wasn't in the greatest of moods, so when he put his hands up on my shoulders as if to hug me - you can only guess my reaction. He said, 'Friend, I took care of your situation with the boy David. I met with his parents and everything is okay. I protected you.' At hearing this, I immediately took a step back and said, 'You're not my friend.'"

Mr. Ryder passed from behind us, holding a double barreled shotgun.

Morales ignored this, and then said, "I then reminded North how once, long ago, that he had told the teachers that he was not our friend, and that I had not forgotten it. I was now merely following his wishes. I then told him that he was not doing his job, because we in essence have no dean. And now teachers like JC, Mr. Ryder, and yourself are left out to dry in the wind. I said, 'Sir, you have left a station unmanned.' But you know what?"

"What?"

"He took *offense* to the words that I was saying! He felt that I was attacking him. He acted nice to my face, but soon I discovered that I had been taken off the list for the teachers who were going to be hired next year! I am a history teacher and did you know that the teacher that they picked over me does not even hold a History degree? I guess that I didn't do enough ass-kissing."

"Right."

"But little did he know that I eat principals like him for breakfast." He then paused, and spit a piece of cud into a cup. "I'm an activist in the Latino community, and I don't back down from a fight. I have gotten two principals fired already, from different schools. I have threatened the School District with law suits several times and won. I am friends with the Superintendent. And I have an appointment with him next week to discuss 'Dr. North.' And I would like you to come with me."

He looked at me directly.

"I'm sorry?"

"You have taken a lot of abuse from these guys, a very lot of abuse. If you were my son I would go after these people with every ounce of firepower I have in these veins."

His words burned right through me, leaving permanent scars. Good scars. Like a Sioux Indian hanging off hooks during the Sundance.

"And I always told my son one thing," he said. "And that is TO STAND UP AGAINST THOSE WHO ABUSE YOU."

This was what I had been needing to hear for a long time. This was the hole that I had in my heart. Of course there was my music, my music which was so much more important to me than a fight I had not picked. *But at some point* ... some point along the way I had learned *not* to fight. I had learned that it was easier to stay *quiet*.

"They have found a way into your doorway," he said, "and now they have taken pepper and poured it on you like you are a fish dead in water. But *no longer* can you stay limp. *No longer* can you not fight. You *must. Your voice must now be heard*, Leo, or *forever will it be closed off.* And ... once you have your first fight, the rest will be easy. It all starts with filing that first petition against them."

I saw that Mr. Hartman had a walkie-talkie in his hand. "Code one, over. Okay, we got Patricia in code blue. Code blue." He looked at Mrs. King. "They're about to do an evaluation on you," he told her. "Better get to your room. Are the dummies set up?"

"Not all of them," she said. "I'll need another."

He tossed her a dummy child from the closet. She flipped a switch on its neck, and the child said, "I love this class."

"Good, it's working," he said. "Here, take this."

JC put the kid over her back. "This is Emmanuel," she told me. "My best student. I actually don't have any normal kids in my classes."

"You don't?"

"No, they're all dummies, like this one."

"See? You fake it all," Anne Marie said. Then she strapped a bomb around her chest and pressed the bright red button.

Morales motioned for me to turn around.

I felt tapping on my left shoulder. It was my good pal from the teacher's lounge.

"Heffel-fleffel-luppogas," Mr. Schendel said. "Now you know," he said, handing me a sword and a chainsaw. "You might need these."

"So what am I supposed to do with these?"

"You hack up your students," he said. "And then replace them, with these dummies."

"Jesus," I said.

"Don't go down without a fight, Heffel-lup-ogas," he said. "We've got your back."

"*Don't go down without a fight*," Mr. Morales said.

When I went to the restroom, I seriously started to ask myself if I was going crazy. But what good were these kids for society, anyway? They were going to work at Smogbusters and pump out more kids like themselves. Most would become hoodlums and prostitutes and stalkers.

When I walked back into Mrs. Fiehr's room, I saw Morales and the rest of the rebellion standing behind him.

"So will you do it, Mr. Heffelapfle? Will you help us fight the administration?" he asked, handing forth a sword and pistol.

I took a deep breath, and then just said it.

"No," I said. "I won't."

The teachers all looked at each other, stunned.

I put on my coat and jacket. Wiped away a tear. They all followed me out to my car.

"Because," I said, getting inside, "what has happened is irredeemable."

"But these people have abused you," said Morales.

"Doesn't everybody."

And I started up my car, and then drove all the way, without stopping, to Portland.

Chapter 40

FINAL THOUGHTS

Of course we both know that there wasn't a gun battle, but that's how it felt. And while I didn't go crazy, that's how it felt. Maybe if Patricia hadn't escaped to the Virgin Islands, I would have come into her office with a machine gun. I just don't know.

But that's how life is. You know, like in that book "No Country for Old Men" – the bad guys often just get away. And those monsters, they are out there, roaming around, parading as normal people.

You want a revenge. You want to take them out. And the anger burns in you every single day, and there's nothing you can do. Except, maybe, hang their picture up in your study and pound nails into their heart and hope it does some damage.

And so I could stay in Vegas, and fight the stalker and the principals and the administration and try to take down the system. But life is short.

I wasn't sad to leave, but Mr. Schendel, Mr. Ryder, and Mr. Hartman sat and ate lunch with me for one last time. And we were very quiet. I had to hold back my tears. I enjoyed our lunches. It would be all that I would miss.

I got up and said I forgot something in my room ... and then, I just kept walking, knowing I'd never see them again.

I sat staring at the kids. Last day of class. Finals day. No popcorn. Maria didn't even show up. But her best friend, Lacey did.

I know this because she was holding up her phone in front of her face and screaming at me, "I'M GOING TO KILL YOU BITCH."

I just stared at her. I mean, I didn't really care.

Ramona, who seemed to obtain power from her voluminous thighs and hips, was the second to lose her mind.

"LISTEN BITCH," she explained, with a real compassionate tone, "YOU'RE FUCKING UGLY ASS TRAILER TRASH NEEDS TO BE BITCHED SLAPPED."

All the girls laughed vociferously.

"Lacey put the phone away or I'll take it away," I said, trying to get the energy to force the air upon my vocal chords. We were beyond needing a cup of coffee. We were beyond going to the gym.

There was going to be another fight after school I heard. Now the girls were obsessed with it, apparently. I looked at Rebecca, the picayune little girl from Brazil. I said to her, "What do you think about all this fighting? It's pretty silly isn't it?"

She responded, demurely, "No. She should beat her ass."

Five more minutes until I never see the students again.

I don't know if I can wait that long.

Now I'm watching them leave.
Reminds me of my last days of school.
Such hope.
Such open vastness of the coming summers.
Leaving.
Freedom.

Ivy, Lancelot, Eddie,
Billy, Manuel, Ramona,
Jessica, Nallely, Mara,

Portia, Angelo, Gary,
Kid Cassidy, Gabino, Rene,
Luis, Adriana, Spencer,
Brian, Alejandra, Monica,
Edgar, Firdnito, Herberto,
Lacey, Jezebel, Roberta,
Maria, Kim, Cassandra,

… all blowing away.
Like dandelion cotton seeds,
into the fields.
I stared at my empty desks.
And then opened my door,
and stepped outside.

EPILOGUE

I drove back up to Montana. In between living at home and in my parents' basement, I lived with some hippies in Missoula. We spent many a night under the cherry tree in the backyard of some random house, playing chess, smoking weed, laughing, and forming a rock group. And as summer wore off I eventually found myself looking for another teaching job. I was hired in Browning, Montana.

I went there only to find the Native American kids in my new classroom were out of control. The teacher whom I was called in to replace had mysteriously quit. When I walked into the class for the first time, the kids were harassing the substitute teacher to the point of tears. There were no books on the shelves - which I took as a bad sign.

"SIT DOWN," I said, with a look of anger.

They had never seen a teacher like me before, some kind of drill sergeant. Little did they know I had just been to boot camp. Since the kids were so out of control, I would have to act like this for the first two months until they learned to respect me, at which I could finally lower my guard.

I went outside and looked up into the sky.

What am I doing?

I thought of the teacher book I had just written.

I'm going in circles. Oh my god. Oh no.

So I did the unthinkable - I turned around, and left.

I literally walked out of the school and drove all the way back to Missoula.

Everyone thought I was crazy.

My parents flipped out.

Sorry, I already did you one favor, Dad.

But I realized, because of the book that I had written, the same book that you're now holding in your very hands, that I had a special insight that nobody else was seeing.

It was only *crazy* if had stayed!

EPILOGUE EPILOGUE

A few years later, I got on the phone and for kicks, I called up my fellow 8th grade teacher, BJ. She was so happy to hear my voice. And she had a lot to say.

"Leo, firstly, that principal was fired right after you left!"

"Really?"

"And Patricia moved," she said.

"Where? Why?"

"I don't know. But that's not the crazy part. Leo, after you left that room, I got put in it. I got put in the hole. Room 445B," she said. "I was there for one year, and guess what happened? I had to quit."

"Why?"

"Because the kids were crazy. On *another* level. *Another* level, Leo! It's like they were insane! They didn't listen to what I was saying. I got every bad kid possible. And the *whole time* I was thinking of you! I was assaulted, a kid hit me and I hit him back. The police got involved. I just tried to make it through the day! I was like, oh my god, this room is haunted. It was like the kids were *possessed*."

"I know! I know!" I shouted, almost crying.

"So I want you to know it wasn't you, Leo. It wasn't you. I've been teaching for 40 years, Leo, and it wasn't you. It was that room. It was the energy in the room."